THE COSMIC PERSPECTIVE

Borgo Press Books by BRIAN STABLEFORD

THE COSMIC PERSPECTIVE

AND OTHER BLACK COMEDIES

by

Brian Stableford

THE BORGO PRESS

An Imprint of Wildside Press LLC

MMIX

CONTENTS

INTRODUCTION

"Dying is easy," the great actor is reported to have said, demonstrating a remarkable flair for stating the obvious; "comedy is hard." Dying is essentially brief, while comedy is essentially sustained, so this is only to be expected.

"Brief" and "sustained" are, of course, relative terms. Some deaths take longer than others, and some kinds of humor generate laughs more rapidly than others. Anecdotal jokes, unlike the quick-fire kind, can afford to string things out and make their audiences wait a little while for the punch-line, but a price always has to be paid for that sort of leisurely approach. Works of humorous fiction that string things out in order to tease, withholding a single laugh-line like a carrot on a stick, not only run the risk of testing the hearer/reader's patience to destruction but also the danger of generating a climactic groan rather than a laugh. The term "shaggy dog story" was not coined as a compliment.

Sustained comedy requires an edge as well as a point, an ongoing flow as well as a terminal twist. It needs to be continually humorous, if not continuously. That is one of the reasons why comic fiction relies so heavy on irony—irony being a *tone*, which requires extension to be properly appreciable—and it is also one of the reasons why comic fiction tends to blackness. A punch-line can sometimes dazzle like a lightning-flash, but continual comedy requires more elaborate chiaroscuro effects, and continuous comedy works better in subtle shades of darkness.

Fortunately for the ironist, and especially the black ironist, fiction has—virtually by definition—a certain intrinsic unreliability.

Fiction is all lies, although it has the virtue, which non-fiction has not, of consisting of honest lies rather than dishonest ones. It is, therefore, fairly easy to adapt the narrative voice of fiction so that it acquires an ironic tone—which is to say, so that its constituent words appear to be saying something other than their literal meaning. Fiction is well-adapted to bluffing, and the essence of comedy—the establishment of expectations that will, at some point, be humorously subverted—is a kind of bluff. Fiction is so well-adapted to bluffing, in fact, that even fiction that is not overtly comic often tends to take on an ironic gloss of its own accord—to the extent that it is sometimes hard to judge whether a story is funny, or, if it is, whether it is intended to be.

I tend to think of all my stories as comedies, partly because I was born without a capacity for sincere belief, and am thus incapable of seeing anything in a wholly serious light, and partly because I am sufficiently cynical to assume that almost all speech acts, and all acts of writing—without any exception—are saying something other than their literal meaning. The stories included here are, however, among the more obvious comedies in my repertoire. This is not to say that nobody dies in them—dying is, after all, far too easy to be omitted from any but the most trivially homespun narratives—but merely that, when characters do die, the reader is not being invited to feel sorry for them, even though they are not actors who are merely pretending, and who can therefore get up again afterwards and make mock-pretentious remarks about how easy it was, compared with getting a laugh.

The humor in the stories tends to the black, in the first place, simply because they are stories; although several of them do have punch-lines, the preparation for those climactic flashes tends to be elaborate and convoluted even in those that are less than a thousand words long, and thus the literary equivalent of a sixty-yard dash. I have to admit, though, that my own sense of humor does tend—excessively, some have been known to opine—to the black. Contrary to the opinion of the aforementioned some, this has little or nothing to do with my cynicism and certainly does not reflect any latent sadism that cannot find expression elsewhere in my placid and humdrum daily existence. It is, I think, a more purely aesthetic matter than that, and has more to do with a distaste for dazzle than a love of shadow *per se*. I have never been a fan of such coarse humorous subgenres as slapstick, innuendo and the comedy of embarrassment; I prefer wit, and cannot understand the point of view that assesses sarcasm as the lowest form of it. For that reason, I have never been able to find anything in the cosmic perspective—whether it aspires to extend the imagination into the macrocosm or any of its counterbalancing microcosms—but black irony.

"The Cosmic Perspective" and "Custer's Last Stand" first appeared in 1985 as the two halves of a back-to-back chapbook, which was the twenty-first in a series issued by the bookseller Chris Drumm. "The Haunted Nursery" first appeared in *A Horror Story a Day: 365 Scary Stories* (Barnes & Noble, 1998) edited by Robert Weinberg, Stefan Dziemianowicz and Martin H. Greenberg. "The Requiem Masque" first appeared in *Albedo One* 3 (Winter 1993) and was subsequently reprinted, along with "The Annual Conference of the Prophets of Atlantis", which first appeared in the *Reminiscon 40 Souvenir Programme* in 1990, in a Necronomicon Press chapbook, *Fables and Fantasies* (1996)."Meat on the Bone" was written for a projected anthology at the request of its editor, Steve Savile, who spent several years sending enthusiastic email messages about the progress of the anthology, including two saying that the contract was in the post, although nothing ever materialized. "Murphy's Grail" first appeared in *Redsine* 4 (February 2001). "Brief Encounter in the Smoking Area" first appeared in *The Interpreter's House* 16 (February 2001). "Fans from Hell" first appeared in *The Steel Caves* December 2000. "The Phantom of Teirbrun" is original to this volume.

THE COSMIC PERSPECTIVE

Henry McCanles was born with a seeming lack of interest in life. It was almost as if he had been stricken, during his sojourn in the womb, with awful doubts as to whether life after birth were possible, and had defensively decided not to pin his hopes upon such a seemingly-bizarre possibility. In infancy, he manifested no exaggerated need for care, protection, security or even love; the pattern of his entire childhood suggested that he was little concerned with the ephemeral pause between birth and death. There never seemed to be a time when his attentions were not directed primarily toward the infinite and the eternal.

At the time of Henry's conception, his father was already over fifty and his mother had just turned forty. At these ages, of course, they were habituated to a life without surprises, and the one that had predicted his arrival was not overwhelmingly welcome. To add to their troubles, Henry was a fortnight overdue, and there were complications. In view of these circumstances, and other coincident factors both social and psychological, it will easily be understood that Henry's oddness was not entirely his own fault, nor entirely his own achievement. It was encouraged in him by many things. The environment of his early life was in no way calculated to impart to him the zest for living that his intrinsic being so obviously lacked.

His parents, before his arrival, had been settling themselves into a peaceful, frozen existence in which they could wait out their lives in comfort and dignity, wasting themselves no further in futile pursuit of dreams they no longer had any hope of attaining. They did their best to continue in this modest ambition in spite of Henry's disruptive presence, and they sucked him into the pattern, albeit without encountering significant resistance. They attained easy command over his needs and desires, effortlessly stifled any demands and the passions that would have prevented the crystallization of their existence, and domesticated him without difficulty. They did not, however, hesitate to make him fully conscious of his status as an intruder and a problem. Henry soon came to conceive of himself not simply as an invader in his own home, but as an outsider in the grand universal design.

His way of life had a good deal in common with the everyday habits of ordinary people, but this was due to mimicry rather than identity. Biologically, Henry McCanles belonged to the same species as the rest of humankind, but in spirit his kinship was more reminiscent of those edible butterflies that drift comfortably through life cunningly disguised as their poisonous competitors, in order that they might escape the attention of predators. Over the years Henry adapted himself meekly and skillfully to the expectations of his parents; he was unobtrusive, never heard and rarely seen, always lost in the rapt contemplation of something outside himself. Such contemplation was always passive, never moving him to activity. Although his parents never grew to consider him a blessing, they accepted him into their scheme of things, and were content.

Henry grew up lean and gaunt, with a pale complexion and an expression of considerable gravity. If he ever sought any kind of amusement or intellectual involvement he did so within himself. It might almost be said that Henry lived his life after birth as a kind of phantom. As he grew older and diversified his associations with the world beyond the walls of home, moving slowly through the education system, he acquired new perspectives on the size, nature and complexity of the known universe. He acquired these perspectives entirely second hand, of course, but he nevertheless became rather fascinated by life and existence in general. His fascination was that of the pure scholar, a non-participant observer. He studied human behavior with the same calm remoteness that he brought to the study of mathematics and the heavens. The study of insect life, the properties of logarithms and the way in which people interacted with one another were all alike to him; there was no sense of personal involvement.

He was thirteen years old when he discovered the stars. The stars had shone in the sky all through his life, and he had observed their presence, but there was still a single climactic moment when, for the first time, he saw something *in* the stars – something meaningful. He looked up one night and, for the first time in his life, experienced a kind of revelation.

Perhaps it was just a moment of carelessness when, because he was alone, his barriers were down. Perhaps it is fated that no man, however slight his engagement with existence, is allowed to tread the course from birth to death without at least one moment of revelation. Either way, thirteen-year-old Henry was struck by a lightning-flash of vision. He looked up, and the stars caught his attention. Then they held it. For some quite unfathomable reason he felt an emotional echo, a sensation, a thrill.

The stars, it seemed then to his immature and rather peculiar mind, lived in the same borderlands of existence as himself. They shared his ability to render themselves unobtrusive. They began to disappear at the slightest hint of atmospheric haziness, and even those strong enough to shine through such hazes were always politely hesitant in their self-assertion.

Henry began to watch and study the stars. It was his first and only hobby. Venus and the moon, he perceived at once, belonged to a different category of being. They shone too confidently. He disowned them. Soon, increasing knowledge of the population of the heavens enabled him to excommunicate Mars, Jupiter and the other planets from the core of his concern. It was the stars that interested him, the stars alone that were *like* him.

He began to cultivate their acquaintance, using—for want of anything better—the methods that had been shown to him at school. He made a few polite inquiries and sought out books to read. It was the inadequacy of what he learned by these means that showed him the fallibility of programmed education. He realized that what he was being taught at school, and the statutory resources that were being made available to him for learning, were of no real relevance to his needs. What he did contrive to discover, however—which was crucial to his requirements—was how to go about constructing a telescope. This he had to do, in order to extend his acquaintance with the stars in the only meaningful way: by extending his perceptions until he was, in a metaphorical sense, among them and intimate with them.

Henry persuaded his parents to part with sufficient money to allow him to purchase, over a relatively short period of time, a large concave mirror, a small plane mirror, and a system of lenses that allowed him to focus on the image in the plane mirror cast by the image in the concave mirror by a tiny sector of sky. He built the frame of the telescope himself, out of odd pieces of wood stolen—"salvaged" might perhaps be a more generous descriptive term—from a local building site.

The instrument was of very limited power, and was really best suited for lunar observation, but Henry's delight—if such a word is not too strong—was to direct the instrument at the Milky Way and thus reveal to his wondering eye the myriad stars that usually hid themselves from human sight.

If Henry had chosen to write his autobiography when he eventually became famous, he would probably have represented the phase that took him from adolescence through higher education and humble employment to incipient middle age as a succession of relationships with astronomical instruments. He progressed from one telescope to another, each time coming a little closer to the infinite by virtue of ever-increasing magnification.

By studying astronomy at university he learned about the variety of stars, and about the evolutionary linkages between the spectral types. He was initiated into the wonders of radio astronomy and x-ray astronomy. He came to understand the mysteries of the galactic red shifts, mastered the arcane mathematics of relativity, involved himself in estimating the ultimate fate of the expanding universe and lost himself in a maze of speculation regarding cosmogenesis, neutron stars, quasars, gamma-ray bursters, black holes, and dark matter. All of that was meat and drink to his increasingly hungry and thirsty mind, not only providing nourishment but exquisite taste sensations.

In graduating from orthodox photography employing optical telescopes to the more complex methods of indirect observation associated with radio astronomy Henry saw himself passing over an important threshold in life, far more important than puberty or the attainment of the age of majority. The surrender of the visual affirmation of his affinity and the removal of his relationship with the stars into a theoretical realm of mathematical purity was a kind of transcendence. Straightforward sensory contact with the objects of his obsession thus became a formality, a matter of occasional convenience. The essence of his love affair became abstract and spiritual, untainted by the vulgarity of mere appearances—which is, according to some commentators, the way all love affairs ought to be. The transition represented a triumph of mind over flesh, intellect over lust.

Henry cultivated the cosmic perspective. To him, the world of human affairs could be meaningful only within the context of the vast and marvelous universe. William Blake had written long before about seeing worlds in grains of sand, heaven in wild flowers, infinity in the palm of one's hand, and eternity in every hour. Henry could see all of these things; in fact, he could not see in any other way. The infinite and the eternal were, to him, far more real than the trivial and brief appearances of mundane existence. The time-scale and the space-scale of the expanding universe were the real yardsticks by which consequence was to be measured, in his view, and the human divisions of seconds and centimeters were mere absurdities.

Radio telescopes provided Henry with the means to gaze, metaphorically speaking, into the farthest reaches of space, and—if the implications of the red-shifts of the most distant quasars were to be believed—across time to the very beginning of the universe. In such remote conceptual realms, Henry lived his real life—but he continued, in the meantime, with some meager fraction of his being, to play the game of mundane existence. He ate and slept, breathed and excreted. Sometimes he wrote papers for publication in journals that hardly anyone read, and occasionally he taught classes in astronomy to students who did not understand what he said and did not care. These things were expected of him. He was expected to earn his living; there were rituals to which he was forced to adhere, in order that he might be allowed to remain in the university milieu that provided him with the means of both physical and mental nutrition. He preserved the life that mattered to him by casual and efficient management of the life that did not.

Such feelings as Henry McCanles had, as he moved about the Earthly world of instruments, observatories and college classrooms, were usually limited to a vague sense of anonymity, but he was occasionally subject to fits of mild depression. He never attempted to fight such attacks of melancholia, nor ever thought of them as anything out of the ordinary, but was content to drift listlessly through them. He was a committed man, but not a blissful one, and would not have known what to say had anyone ever asked him whether he was happy—which, in fact, no one ever did. He tended to wear his customary indifference without embarrassment or apology.

The people who worked alongside him—indeed, all those whose lives touched the periphery of his in any way at all—could sometimes be disarmed by the pathos that he radiated when he descended further into depression than was usual, but they did not even trouble to offer him advice. He was not a difficult man to get along with, being always courteous, cool and unassuming. He was a good listener, because he did listen, even though the information he obtained by this means made no impact upon him. Although he was not aware of the fact, other people occasionally contrived to become quietly fond of him *via* the occasional exercise of pity and kindness, although they rarely gave voice to their fondness and never attempted to demonstrate it in action. Others regretted his loneliness, even if he did not, but they let him be, because that seemed to be the right thing to do. No one in the world had anything against him, except for a few petty professional jealousies that arose because he was so meticulous in his work that he never made mistakes himself, and sometimes exposed the mistakes of others.

There is nothing surprising in the fact that so many people liked Henry, in spite of the fact that he seemed unable to like them. Despite all that cynics say, it is quite usual for people who can do it to feel fond of other people. A surprisingly high proportion of the human race actually yearn—at least some of the time—to feel fond of other people, and only become embittered if they feel that the opportunity is being unfairly denied them. Some few of the remainder succeed in finding targets for their wayward affections routinely, but become disillusioned by the effects that fondness tends to have, and gradually lose the incentive. Henry McCanles was one of the rare people who not only provided useful raw material for the sympathies of others by remaining available, but was also so totally unaffected by such sympathies that the risk of their getting out of hand, or being perverted into something more powerful, was remote. However, as every gambler knows, unlikely events do sometimes happen, and it happened that among the many fond feelings that Henry attracted to himself were the particular fond feelings of Stella Joyce, which did indeed become gradually exaggerated into something more like obsession than mere camaraderie.

Henry was then working at one of the better universities in the American South, where he enjoyed convenient access to one of the world's largest radio telescopes, good computation facilities and an excellent library. Everything he required was at his disposal, including abundant assistance in many of the more tedious aspects of evidential collation. Stella Joyce was one of his post-graduate students. He never noticed her at all during working hours, where she was simply an instrument to be used according to the rules of the game. Had there been no opportunity for the two of them to meet outside working hours, there would have been little possibility of his ever becoming aware of her existence as an independent human being. Some such opportunities did arise, however. Henry, like other mortals, had to eat, and he took his meals in the most convenient refectory, along with several hundred students and those members of staff whose own domestic situations made such measures necessary. This rendered him available for anyone wishing to cultivate his acquaintance outside the professional context.

Stella began to follow the simple strategy of waiting for him to collect his meal and sit down to eat it, and then going to sit beside him. Stella's interest in astronomy was actually fairly slight, although she was sufficiently intelligent and capable in her studies to have qualified for postgraduate study. She had been encouraged into the field by unfortunate and misguided pressure applied by her mother, who was a devoted follower of horoscopes and thought that a bright future must await any girl with an intimate knowledge of the stars and their ways. As with so many simple believers, Stella's mother could not comprehend the difference between astronomy and astrology, but Stella was nevertheless content with her ill-chosen vocation. Knowledge of any sort was of little importance to her; she depended far more on her emotions to determine the quality of her life. It was her emotions—which were no more directed by reason than her choice of career—that guided her to Henry McCanles. She fell in love with him, honestly and sincerely, and as deeply as she could.

Such fancies are not uncommon, but they often remain dormant when they receive no encouragement and generally fizzle out eventually even if they do. In all probability, other female students had toyed with the idea of seducing Professor McCanles, but few such whims had ever generated more than tokenistic exploratory action; Stella was the only one who persisted, even after realizing that the mission seemed virtually impossible. Had she been willing to side-track her infatuation, to sublimate it into part of the fantasy component of her private imaginative existence, the course of history might have been subtly altered—but she did not.

Perhaps, like her mother, Stella Joyce had some latent but unassailable faith in the notion that the future is predetermined, and considered that Henry and she were indeed star-crossed. It was more likely, though, that other causal factors were more significant in determining her persistence. She was twenty-three, and her infatuation with Henry was by no means the first time she had been "in love". It was, however, the first time that such love had not rebounded on her with unexpected promptitude in an ugly and painful manner. She was a virgin who had suffered considerable social deprivation in her childhood by virtue of chronic myopia. Forced to wear spectacles from the age of five, she had never liked them, and had often removed them once she was out of her mother's protective sight, with the inevitable result that her interaction with the world around her had been dogged by the difficulty of an inability to perceive much of it. This difficulty had only been overcome, in the usual manner, a few months before she fell in love with Henry.

Henry, of course, remained unaware of the infatuation. It did not seem to him to be significant that Stella materialized at his elbow with startling regularity while he primed his organism with fuel. Her attempts at flirtation—the shy fluttering of unpracticed sexual wings—passed him by. He was always polite and pleasant, never, even by the slightest word or gesture, either reciprocating or explicitly rejecting her tentative emotional advances. She therefore persisted, not only in attempting to build a more intimate relationship, but also in believing that she was succeeding.

Henry accepted her company gracefully. He made no attempt to disassociate himself. Stella's company at meals, her conversation, and, ultimately, her evening visits to his room, slowly became a habit. Stella was, wisely, physically undemanding. She never attempted even a kiss, but was simply content to be with him, to be a part of his life. She was careful not to be a nuisance, taking from him only such time as could be easily surrendered by his work.

In effect, Stella Joyce married Henry McCanles by degrees. Inch by inch, she crept into his routine, co-opting one by one the supportive tasks that Henry found so cumbersome, which could so conveniently be translated into wifely duties. She began cooking for him, shopping for him, and planning his quotidian schedules for him. She took him over. Even so, the relationship might never have come to full fruition had it not been for one singular fact. Stella might never have eased Henry out of his deep rut to the extent of attaining the climax of an actual wedding had it not been for the fact that, in a most curious manner, Henry eventually fell in love with her.

Actually, it would be more correct to say that Henry fell in love with a twinkle in Stella's eye. He first saw the twinkle when they were sitting at supper one night in his apartment, facing one another, with the table between them and the electric light overhead and slightly to the side. He saw a gleam in her right eye that looked exactly like a star. It winked, and then disappeared as she turned her head.

As time went by, Henry caught glimpses of the star again, always brief and strangely frustrating. Sometimes it appeared in one eye, sometimes the other, but never in both simultaneously. He found, over a period of weeks, that the light inevitably appeared for a brief moment or two when the position of her head made a certain angle with the sun or some artificial light-source. The angle had to be exact, and the merest turn of the head would destroy it; he soon calculated its value in degrees of arc, but regarded the result as a mere datum, never interrogating its potential significance. The star fascinated him.

This was not a revelation, to be compared with his first discovery of the stars in the sky, but it was a discovery. It was something new, something attractive, something that had to be followed up. It was, after all, a star of some sort, more fugitive than any in the night sky, its hold on existence apparently so much more precarious. It seemed to Henry to be quite lovely.

Henry did not have the force of personality that would have been required to take positive steps every day or every night in order to conjure up the tremulous silver gleam. He was, instead, content to wait and watch, to study Stella as she talked and moved in her carefully tentative fashion through their relationship, always alert and ready to catch the glimmer as it shimmered into existence and just as rapidly shivered out. Because of that single star, Henry was ready to accept when Stella finally plucked up enough courage to propose marriage. He had, by then, an adequate motive for taking such a step. He would probably never have proposed it himself, but he was ready when the proposal came, and he accepted it with a good grace.

Stella never knew anything about the trick of light that had offered her the captivity of Henry's heart and soul. She was not so slow-witted as to imagine that Henry lusted after her body with any particular fervor, or that he had any considerable admiration for her brain, but she thought that she could be everything he could ever want or need in a wife, and she foolishly imagined that her own love could outlast any trial or tribulation.

Stella made all the arrangements for the wedding, with due discretion and taste. Henry patiently waited out the formal engagement and the preparations for their union, up to and including the ceremony. Every now and then, he caught a glimpse of the tantalizing star; the sight always reassured him that, not only was he playing the game honestly and fairly, but also that he was going to win his prize and keep his trophy. The star in Stella's eyes beguiled him almost as much as the mysterious radio signals from the edge of the universe, even though he found his analytical methods inadequate to its comprehension. He could never hope to measure either its right ascension or its red shift, and could not properly track its variability. His observational means were scientifically incompetent, for the moment, but he could at least maintain the star within the orbit of his observation—or so he thought.

There was no sexual component to the pre-marital relationship, and it was with mildly anxious feelings of anticipation and trepidation that Henry realized, on his wedding night, that Stella intended him to make love to her. He had, of course, considered this particular aspect of husbandly duty previously, but had always decided to cross the bridge when he came to it. As he actually approached it, though, he felt an entirely natural twinge of fear.

He got into bed first and lay there, waiting for Stella to join him. Only by recalling books that he had read many years before could he plan what was required of him, and, as he recalled them, the sense of strangeness and vague disgust that had attended that particular aspect of his early reading returned to him with some force. Nevertheless, because it was part of the game he had consented to play, he composed himself with care and deliberation. He had every intention of going through with the performance, even though his vulnerability to the slings and arrows of outrageous fortune was, at that particular moment, greater than it had been in the previous forty years.

Stella eventually emerged from the bathroom and came to kiss him on the mouth before getting into bed beside him. He was rewarded, then, by a glimpse of the mysterious star, and it seemed that all might be well.

Then tragedy struck.

If only Stella had used the privacy of the bathroom to perform *all* the rituals of preparing for bed, the dangerous moment might have passed safely—but she, like Henry, was very much a creature of habit, and there was one small operation that she *always* performed while sitting in bed—the last action of each and every day.

She knew of no reason why she might need to alter this particular aspect of her routine.

And so, while Henry watched, she carefully removed the contact lenses from her short-sighted eyes.

Henry realized, in a blinding flash of sickening inspiration, what the star in Stella's eyes really was.

The star was not a part of Stella at all. It was only an optical illusion—a reflection in the tiny slivers of glass or plastic whose existence he had never suspected. Had he ever really looked closely at Stella's eyes, he surely would have realized, but he never had. He had only looked at and for the star…the faint, superficial ghost of a remote source of radiance. Only now did he discover that it was, in fact, an item of deception, like a seeming specter that turned out to be a flapping sheet.

He said nothing. His face did not betray by the slightest shift of expression that his spirit had received, in this most sensitive of matters, at a moment of unprecedentedly high tension, a shattering blow. His body, alas, being far less subject to conscious control, could not help but testify to his distress. He was impotent, and so he was to remain throughout his marriage.

The marriage staggered on for two years, while Stella tried hard—but all in vain—to maintain her own affections in the face of such cruel adversity. She gave the marriage everything she had to give, but, after that one crucial setback, it seemed that she less and less to offer. In the meantime, what Henry had to offer her came to seem like nothing at all. There was no hope for the relationship, in the long run. It was no one's fault. It simply happened that way.

In the end, Stella carefully unmade all the arrangements that she had so carefully made, engineered an amicable divorce with the same patience she had put into engineering the amicable marriage, took back her maiden name, and went her own way in life. She gave up astronomy for good, without a pang of regret. It would not be fair to say that she was no worse for the experience, but it did not take her long to recover.

During those two years Henry descended gently into one of his shallow depressions, but this time he never came out of it. He worked on with the same calm efficiency, and the same seeming indifference to his surroundings. The instruments and methods of his inquiry did not change at all, so it was not obvious to anyone around him that he was now working form a slightly different observational standpoint. He looked at the stars, now, with slightly different eyes. He brought to their study a subtly different kind of imagination—and during those two years, in the wake of the wedding-night disaster and its long aftermath, he formulated the theory that was to make him famous and change the course of human destiny.

Henry gathered all his evidence with the utmost care. He weighed it, analyzed it precisely, and built it into an impressive edifice of unmistakable implication. Then, using predictions generated by his theoretical equations, he went on to check every item of data, and every step of his logic, using observations made by a host of others as well as his own. By the time he published his results, the case he made was quite perfect.

Henry's thesis was that the cosmos contained no matter whatsoever outside the solar system—that the shell of the universe itself was only a short distance beyond the Oort Cloud, and that all the stars and galaxies—every point of light, every single source of electromagnetic signals—were the products of optical illusion. The vast expanding universe, according to Henry, was nothing but a pattern of reflected gleams of sunlight, hideously distorted into all kinds of lying implications by a spherical "lens" of stressed and convoluted space that englobed the heliocentric system.

According to Henry McCanles, *all* was illusion.

Had the notion come from a crank, it would never have reached cold print, but it did not come from a crank. It came from a man known to be the most careful, able and dedicated astronomer in the world. It came supported with a multitude of data and an elaborate web of impeccable calculations. Henry's theory not only explained all the anomalies of classical theory—the nature of the quasars, the question of the origin of the universe, the ambiguous relationship between red shift and distance—by means of a mathematical model of the stressed shell, but it made a whole series of predictions which, if the theory were false, could be falsified.

Other cosmologists were quick to respond, if only because they wanted to dispose of the absurd new model in the briefest possible time. There was not a single theorist anywhere in the world who gave the least credit to the model, in the beginning, but there was not a single one who could find a scrap of evidence to refute it. Many still refused to believe it, even in the absence of evidence, claiming that such a thing simply could not be, but a growing number were impressed by the self-consistency of Henry's theory, by the man himself, and by the way in which all their tentative objections were met with mathematical grace and perfection.

Gradually, other astronomers, physicists and cosmologists began to admit the possibility of distorted spatial fabric that refracted and tangled light rays in exactly the way Henry said it did. Laboratory experiments were set up, sometimes at great expense, to investigate whether space really could be distorted and the basic constants of the universe altered in concert. Some of the experiments demonstrated the existence of such potential, and the failure of those that did not was rapidly explained by the growing party of Henry's supporters. Henry's thesis also began to gather popular credence and approval.

Many people, it turned out, had never been comfortable with the size of the universe as calculated by twentieth century astronomers. It was too vast, too intimidating, too challenging. A compact universe seemed somehow more human: a more appropriate womb for matter, life and emotion.

While he was going through the laborious motions of his divorce, Henry McCanles first became the most notorious scientist who had ever lived, and then the most famous and feted. He was the ultimate iconoclast—the man who had proved that the whole vast universe discovered by twentieth century science was a hollow myth—and his reputation followed a familiar trajectory. At first resented and reviled, he was then lauded and declared a hero. Unlike many iconoclasts unlucky enough to be born into a world where things moved more slowly, though, he made the transition in a matter of months. He did not have to die before being taken seriously.

The world adapted with amazing rapidity to Henry's revelations, and gave them the welcome they deserved. Everyone but a few diehard traditionalists stuck in the mud of mental indolence accepted that the solar system was an existential fragment trapped like a fly in amber within the cocoon of a quintessential lens, and that infinity had never been anything but a human delusion of grandeur. The imaginative horizons of the human race collapsed like a punctured balloon, and came back down to Earth with a splutter. Humankind's image of itself was seriously and significantly changed, seemingly for the better. Thankfully, there were no longer more things in heaven and earth than were dreamt of in human philosophy. The universe was no longer stranger than humans could imagine, or even stranger than humans *did* imagine. All of sudden, whatever their faults might be, humans really were the crowning glory of creation. There was one Earth, one sun, and a litter of dead rocks—such was the extent of the material world.

Several eminent rivals, inevitably, accused Henry bitterly of taking science back two thousand years, to the days of Aristotle's closed world and crystal spheres—but others pointed out that it was in that image that the true harmony of the spheres, as described by Aristotle's mentor, Plato, had always resided. Centuries of human imaginative endeavor, the envious claimed, had been laid waste at a single stroke—and a good thing too, Henry's supporters said. How much more valuable time might have been wasted in arcane quasi-alchemical dabblings with incomprehensible and futile illusions? Henry's own triumph was soon followed by others of a similar stripe, which demonstrated that the bizarre microcosm of quantum mechanics was equally illusory, and that atoms were really tiny transparent spheres closely akin to the macrocosmic sphere that enclosed them, and just as deceptive.

The day that Henry's divorce was finalized was, coincidentally, the day on which he had been invited to address the largest gathering of the world's scientists ever assembled in one place. He had already declined that invitation, as he had declined all others; he preferred to let the written word speak for him, and was content to leave public performance, idolatry and controversy to people who liked those sorts of things. He felt that he had done his work, and had no wish either to mourn the fate of obsolete paradigms or dance on their grave.

He had resigned his post at the University a few days before, and had decided to indulging himself in an unprecedented breach of etiquette by not working out his period of notice. Instead, when the divorce papers delivered in the morning mail confirmed that he was single again, he set out to drive his unobtrusive car into the desert, only pausing en route at a suburban supermarket to buy a revolver. He intended to find a quiet spot where he could blow his brains out without seriously inconveniencing anyone.

He was not quite sure why he intended to commit suicide, but it somehow seemed to be a good idea, in aesthetic if not in moral terms. He told himself that the decision had nothing to do with the divorce, nor with the fact that, by radically changing his fellow human beings' concept of their relationship with the universe he had significantly altered the course of history. He simply felt, without reasoning it through, that his life was over and that there was nothing left for him to do but end it swiftly and neatly.

Henry parked the car just off the highway, at a conveniently remote location, loaded the gun, and then got out. He locked all the doors and checked the trunk. He replaced the keys in his pocket and began walking south, into the great wasteland. He walked for about an hour, until the road and the car were no longer visible, and the sound of the distant traffic had been reduced to a vague and distant murmur that might have been the hum of insects. By this time, it was late evening. He sat down in the shadow of an outcrop of tawny rock, in order to watch the stars come out.

He had not intended to linger over the business of self-disposal, but his hand seemed curiously reluctant to raise the barrel of the pistol in order to direct it at his skull. He realized, while he paused, that it was a long time since he had actually looked up at the stars with his naked eyes, in rapt contemplation of their glory. That glory had been theoretically eroded, of course—practically destroyed, since he had exposed them for the lies that they were—but in purely visual terms, the stars were exactly what they had always been, just as tantalizing and frustrating as ever. They were only optical illusions, no longer unduly mysterious, but they were still fascinating, in their fashion—and while he watched them emerge in the clear desert sky, it struck him quite forcibly that they were still quite beautiful. There was something about them that he could not quite specify or analyze, in spite of all his triumphant calculations. Strangely enough, they seemed unfamiliar, even though there was no man on Earth more familiar with their disposal and their true nature than he was.

Perhaps, he thought, it had been so long since he had last renewed sensory contact with the objects of his affection that he had forgotten the actual and immediate *effect* of staring up into the reaches of the night sky.

Nostalgia meant nothing to Henry McCanles, but something stirred in his veins while his eyes dwelt upon the stardust ribbon of the Milky Way, and his mind's eye drew constellation patterns among the brighter lights. It might have been sentiment, but it was more likely a touch of vulgar madness.

A snake, resting in a crevice at the base the outcrop of rock, was roused from its patient inertia by the proximity of warm-blooded flesh. It moved out into the open, its scales rustling like silk over the rough surface of the sand. Henry heard it, and looked down. In the darkness, he took it for a rattlesnake, although it was not. He also imagined that it spoke to him, and immediately assumed that the voice he heard was the voice of God. Needless to say, it was not—but Henry presumably needed to hear the voice of God right at that moment, and improvised as best he could.

"What do you want?" was what Henry imagined the voice of God saying to him.

His immediate impulse was to inform God that he had come out to seek oblivion through the customary channels, but he changed his mind. "This was all *your* doing," was what he finally said. His voice was colorless, without any trace of anger or spite.

"True," admitted the snake.

"You created it: the illusion; all the illusions. You made me fall in love with the stars, and with Stella. You fooled us all into thinking there was an infinite universe with countless suns and countless worlds, and love too. You encouraged us believe that we were part of something *big*—something truly important—but there was only us. Humankind. Stella and me. One sun, and a few lumps of rock floating round it. A pair of contact lenses. Nothing *real*."

God did not bother to point out the several minor inaccuracies in this unusually heartfelt statement. Instead, He said: "For most of their history, people have believed there was only Earth, with a few lights scattered in the sky. It made them feel important. Then they came to believe that there was a lot more. That made them feel clever. Now they believe that there really is only Earth, after all, and a few lights scattered in the sky, and they feel important as well as clever. It's all good, all progress. I've always been in favor of progress, whatever people say."

"It's not progress," Henry replied, "and it's not good. We can't ever recover the kind of innocence we once had. We had the illusion, we fell for it, and then we lost it. It can't ever be the same again. We glimpsed infinity and we believed in it. We did all we could to encompass it in our imagination, but now we have to stop and go back again. The divorce is final now. How do you close an open mind?"

"I don't know," said God. "I never had such a thing. Are you quite sure that you did?"

"Why did you do it?" asked Henry.

"Why did *you*?" countered God. "It was you who made the discoveries, you who proved impotent, you who told the world and became famous. You appointed yourself as a messiah—that wasn't my doing. To tell you the truth, Henry, you wouldn't have been my first choice. You're too dull, and you have more than a hint of lunacy about you."

"Whose fault is that?" asked Henry, flatly, but with a hint of sarcasm.

"That's right," said the snake. "You can always blame me. I make a great scapegoat."

They might have argued about that for hours, but Henry was beginning to find the imaginary conversation a bit wearing. He tried to get back to the point by saying: "You still haven't told me why you did it."

"Does it matter?" said God.

"You're not a great one for answering questions, are you?" commented Henry.

"No," admitted the snake. "It was never one of my strong points—but I can certainly ask them. *Does* it matter?"

"It does to me," said Henry.

"Whose fault is that?" countered God.

They could have argued about that for a long time, too, if Henry had had the energy. He didn't.

"I believed in it," said Henry. "I really did. I believed in a vast and wonderful universe, in something rich and complex, in a universe of unlimited possibility, of unimaginable potential—but it was all a lie: the universe and life alike. Because you couldn't be bothered. Because you couldn't make a universe like that. All you could manage was a sun and an Earth and some loose debris, all wrapped up in a crinkly piece of wrapping material."

"Aristotle liked it," said the snake. To Henry, that seemed like a remark of unparalleled irrelevance—but he knew that God was letting him down gently. The truth was that almost everybody liked it. Henry didn't—but he had always been a misfit.

"I was going to shoot myself," Henry said, "but now I've met you, I can't see that there's any need. Here's my hand. Bite me."

So saying, Henry transferred the pistol from his right hand to his left, and held the right hand close to the snake's mouth, inviting it to strike.

"Certainly," said God, and bit the hand that was not attempting to feed Him.

God was not, however, poisonous. The snake was harmless, and its teeth barely scratched Henry's skin. He sat and nursed the hand for some minutes, waiting for the agony to begin, while the snake retreated apprehensively to its crevice. Nothing happened. Henry didn't even feel giddy.

"It's all a cheap trick, isn't it?" asked Henry, sounding genuinely bitter for the first time. "Even this is just a cheap trick." The scratch was hardly bleeding.

"I don't know," said the snake, from a safe distance. "You tell me."

"I'll tell you what," said Henry. "I'll make a deal with you. Send me back in time to the moment of my birth so that I can start all over again...and I'll try to do better."

"Not exactly generous with the incentives, are you?" the snake observed. "Besides which, it's just not on. The trouble with you humans is that you want everything easy: mechanical; straightforward;

laid on. Well, it's not. You have to start from where you are. Common sense tells you that. No second chances."

"From where I am?" said Henry. "Newly divorced from a marriage I couldn't consummate? In a universe no bigger than a comet's orbit? In a life full of nothing but tarnished illusions? Don't you think that's asking of a lot from a weak sort of individual like me?"

"Certainly," said God, deigning to answer a question for once.

Henry sat still for two more minutes. Then he looked up into the sky. The stars were still shining. They were still beautiful. Like a Rembrandt that had turned out to be a fake, they had lost their glamour, their mystique and their presumed value in the marketplace of the imagination, but they still looked just as good. They were some forgery. Looked at dispassionately, they were about as romantic as electric lights reflected in a contact lens, but they were still there.

The snake, perhaps feeling, in his role as stand-in for God, that all decisions could now be left safely in Henry's hands, slid out of sight into the utmost depths of the crevice.

Henry, realizing that he was all alone again, suddenly remembered another question.

"Hang on a minute," he called, speaking aloud for the first time. "Is there life after death?"

The question echoed in the night, disturbing the comfortable silence that was now undisturbed even by the hum of insects, or anything similar. Somewhere, out of sight, the snake eventually hissed. Somewhere in the hiss, Henry imagined that God was saying: "Use your imagination."

It was not the answer for which he had hoped, but he had to admit that it was probably correct.

Henry walked back to the car and drove back into town. He stopped off at the supermarket to claim a refund on the gun, and used the cash to buy groceries. As he left the store he smiled at the cashier, who blinked back at him, perhaps mistaking his intentions, in a conspicuously myopic fashion.

"You should have your eyes tested and get some spectacles," he advised her. "The world would be in focus then, and you'd know what you've been missing."

The cashier studiously ignored the remark, but he knew that she was probably thinking that he ought to mind his own business.

THE HAUNTED NURSERY

The Englishman, the Scotsman, and the Irishman agreed that they would take turns to enter the haunted nursery and make every effort to stay there all night. They each put £100 into the pot; the one who contrived to remain in there for the longest time would scoop the pool. They cut cards to decide who would go first, and the Englishman drew the lowest.

After twenty-five minutes, the Englishman was back in the drawing-room, pouring himself a very large brandy.

"That's no ordinary haunted room," he told the Scotsman and the Irishman. "I met the Devil himself. That wouldn't have been so bad if I'd been able to face up to him man-to-man, but I wasn't. The moment I looked at him I was thirteen again, in my first term at Eton, fagging for that sadistic bastard Harding. He made my life a living hell, you know—I can't go into details. A living hell. It was worse than the army—worse than the Gulf, far worse than Belfast before the cease-fire—because I wasn't *equipped.* I wasn't trained. There's only one thing worse than being thirteen in a living hell, and that's *going back* to being thirteen in a living hell—being stripped of all the adult equipment, all the training, being reduced to absolute helplessness and *knowing* just how pathetically and ridiculously helpless you are. I'd forgotten it all, buried it and blanked it out—but *he* brought it all back again. I could endure having my eyes plucked out, but not that."

The Scotsman and the Irishman had a good laugh about that before the Scotsman took his own turn in the haunted nursery.

He was back in the drawing-room twenty-five minutes later, pouring himself a huge whisky.

"Same bloody thing," he said, in his terse Scottish manner. "Devil in disguise. I wor nae but six year old an' ma bloody da had his bloody belt off again. Blubbin' like a babe, I was. All ma life I've been tellin' maesel' that if ever I'd got holt o' that bastard when we were two of a size I'd ha' kicked the shit out o'him an' spat on the wreck—but I wor nae but six year old and there was nithin' I could do while that brass buckle came down an' down an' down agin. Nithin' at all—an' I *remembered* everythin' I'd forgot about all o' that stuff. Every bloody thing I'd buried an' blanked. I could'ae taken havin' ma eyes plucked out, but no' that. No' that."

This time, it was only the Irishman who laughed. As the Irishman went off to the haunted nursery to take his turn, the Englishman said to the Scotsman: "Do you think he has sense or sensitivity enough to be taken the same way?"

"I give him ten minutes," the Scotsman said, grimly. "Not a bloody minute more."

The Irishman came back after exactly ten minutes. He poured himself a modest glass of whiskey and sipped it delicately, as if he'd never tasted it before. Then he turned to his adversaries.

"Twas the Divvil all right," he said. "Hisself in all his foul an' fire-an'-brimstone glory, just like the Faithers up at Saint Pat's used to tell us. Never thought to see the like. Four years old, I thought I was, before me first communion—an' lookin' the Divvil hisself in the burnin' yeller eye." He stopped, and took another appreciative sip from his glass.

"And then what?" said the Englishman, breathlessly wanting to hear the gory details before he and the Scotsman split the pot.

"I just said 'How d'ye do, Musther Divvi, it must be awful dull an' lonely stuck in this pokey little room fer all eternity. Would ye like to swap bodies wi' me for a little while, so that I can win a bet against a Presbyterian an' a public schoolboy?' An' the Divvil said 'Sure'—an' here he is."

And the Irishman—or whatever was wearing his body just then—reached out with one clawed hand to pluck out the anxious eyes of the Englishman and the Scotsman, while the other collected the £300.

THE PHANTOM OF TEIRBRUN

I.

In the days before the great city of Is was swallowed up by the sea, the port had a number of satellite towns, all of which were thought by their citizens to be places of importance by virtue of their proximity to such a notorious place. One of these was the ancient walled town of Teirbrun, whose citizens were extremely proud of the antiquity of their residence—which, they claimed, dated back to the times when Is had been a mere fishing-port named Ys and the great forest of Leonais had been a royal hunting-ground whose name was spelled Lyonesse. Their disapproval of Is was entrenched long before the great city acquired its reputation as the most reprehensible sink of iniquity west of Byzantium, and was always expressed in terms of an exaggerated regard for the niceties of morality and the sternness of the legal retribution.

In fact, the citizens of Teirbrun were not particularly moral by the standards of Leonais, nor did the town's watchmen and constables contrive to arrest a greater proportion of common law-breakers than any town of comparable size within the province, but those law-breakers who were apprehended and brought to trial there were often punished with greater ferocity. When a crime was committed for which no perpetrator could be identified, that circumstance always excited a great deal of angry complaint and bitter criticism of the town authorities.

This ostentatious respect for the law and eagerness to see it properly enforced led the noblemen and merchants of Teirbrun to be exceedingly particular in their attitude to the rights of property and crime of theft. Whenever the town's mayor had to give a speech to a select company of the men who had put him in his office, he was always took care to assure them—even though the assertion was unsupported by much evidence—that there was nowhere else in Bretagne where property was safer, that this safety resulted from the fact that thieves were nowhere so fearful of the rewards of judgment as they were in Teirbrun, and that there was no other town in the entire kingdom in which the scaffolds were so frequently hung with the broken bodies of already-handless miscreants who had dared to repeat such heinous offences as stealing a loaf of bread or poaching a rabbit.

In view of the enthusiasm with which its people publicly expressed their respect for morality and the law, an innocent visitor might have imagined that Teirbrun was an exceptionally happy and orderly town. The people of Bretagne have, however, always been inclined to discontent and disorder, and there were many among Teirbrun's common inhabitants—especially among the ungrateful poor—who were embittered by the pretensions of their masters, and resentful of the various ways in which ostentatious attempts at rigorous law-enforcement of the law inhibited their spirit of adventure.

"How could we live if stealing were to become impracticable?" some ragged townsmen would often remark to one another, when the two happened to meet in one of their secret dens of vice or filthy taverns. "Would we be obliged to go back to the land, to spoil our hands and break our backs in the planting and the reaping? What are towns for but to gather property together in cupboards and strongboxes, so that its redistribution might be facilitated?"

"What possible benefit would we obtain from going back to the land?" his friend would observe. "The best grain goes to the rich, who neither dig nor pick, and the people who work the fields are left with the turnips and the beets."

"Nor is it practicable for us to seek work as watchmen or constables," the first would add, "for we are the ones for whom watchmen need to watch and constables must chase, and our new masters would soon perceive that we had nothing to do if we were to become traitors to our own cause."

On the rare occasions when they had coin enough to get thoroughly drunk, these shoeless philosophers sometimes became bold. "We need to reclaim the night for those who have stealthy business to conduct," they would proclaim "We ought to discover among our ranks a robber of true daring, who can thumb his nose at the mayor and his magistrates, and defy every effort made by the constables, the watchmen and the militia to bring him down. We need a hero."

Alas, as is so often the way with drunken proclamations, these stirring words were usually forgotten by the time dawn broke; time after time, appeals to the patron saint of pilferers went unheard, despite being elaborately clad in alcoholic eloquence, and years passed while no robber of true daring emerged to play the hero and recover the night for the fearful thieves of Teirbrun. In fact, the town's underdogs knew only too well that no such paragon of cleverness was ever likely to be found among their ranks. When winter came to Bretagne, Teirbrun's poor folk grew lean, and many became less capable in their various imaginary trades as they were caught in risky business and returned to their families lightened by a hand.

The day did eventually dawn, however, when a series of robberies commenced in Teirbrun that caused a sensation, and relit the flame of hope that the dead hand of the law had extinguished in the town's most wretched homes. The robberies in question were not petty thefts of food, household implements and underclothing from the marketplace, nor even a matter of the skillful cutting of fat purses. They were burglaries of the boldest kind: the work of a daring housebreaker, who was able to scale high walls and pick sturdy locks. He not only carried away jewels and coins but bottles of fine wine, cheeses, instruments of household discipline—whips, scolds' bridles and the like—and magical objects of every description, and he seemed to have a particular fondness for daggers and pistols.

Only a handful of the people who were robbed in the early days of the burglar's career caught so much as a glimpse of this menace to society, and they were unable to offer a useful description of him. All that they were able to report to the constables was that he went about his business cloaked in black, and that he wore a black silk mask to hide his face.

The only person came near to laying hands upon the mysterious thief in those early days was a fat grocer, who was at the time clad only in a linen nightshirt, and he lost all further enthusiasm for a tussle when he discovered that the thief was armed with an exceedingly sharp and stout dagger, whose blade was razor-sharp on both sides. The robber used this weapon—which was more a poniard than a mere dagger, according to the grocer's testimony—to slice through the nightshirt from top to bottom with a single casual sweep, exposing the honest tradesman's belly and unmentionables, albeit without shedding a single drop of blood.

"He stole the bag of coins that contained my life savings and the best stock from my larder," wailed this unlucky man, when he told his anxious friends of his terrible ordeal, "and he did not hesitate to add insult to injury when I confronted him and cursed him as a truffle-digging pig, for he took my powdered wig from my nightstand and impaled it on a spike upon my gate as he left the premises."

In another realm, the grocer's audience might have laughed about the wig; in Bretagne, however, a merchant who apes the nobility by playing the fop is not reckoned a figure of fun, at least by his own kind. The fact that the robber carried such a deadly weapon was taken very seriously, for it was held to be clear proof of his murderous intent, and rich men began to quiver in their beds for fear that the thief might puncture more than their wigs.

Within a matter of weeks, every man of quality in the town who had not yet been visited by the master-thief was fearful that his turn to be robbed would come soon enough, and a howling chorus began imploring the mayor for adequate protection. "Such horrors are doubtless an everyday occurrence in the dreadful city of Is," they cried, "but this is ancient Teirbrun, where the law is legendary for its firmness and the peace has been sternly kept for a hundred years. This kind of thing cannot be tolerated."

The mayor soon became desperate as his popularity plummeted, but the strenuous efforts to which he roused the watchmen, constables and the militia were all to no avail. It was evident—to the beleaguered mayor, at least—that stronger measures would have to be taken. "This is some kind of phantom that is plaguing us," the mayor informed an extraordinary meeting of the Town Council. "He is evidently no merely human robber, but a black magician, who is able to evade our every precaution by means of cunning spells! We must petition the Church to send us a skilled witchfinder to deal with the phenomenon!"

The Councillors were not entirely convinced by the mayor's conclusion, but they could see the wisdom of it. They were, in some sense, responsible for the failures of the watchmen, the constables and the militia, but they could not be held responsible for the failure of an expert witchfinder. Unfortunately, when they petitioned the Archbishop, he replied that his witchfinders were far too busy identifying members of murderous heretical cults and tracking down witches' sabbats to be distracted by mere matters of common theft—but he did agree to send an investigator to make a careful analysis of the situation, in order to determine whether there were indeed diabolical forces at work. No one in Teirbrun had much confidence in the outcome of such an investigation, but the fact that they had issued the appeal meant that they were forced to pay for the accommodation and feeding of the investigator—who turned out to be a short, stout Benedictine monk named Odo—and treat him with due deference.

Rumor of the mayor's judgment that supernatural forces were at work reached the houses of the poor some time before the news of the Archbishop's response—which, when it eventually came, redoubled the merriment thus generated. From that moment on, the robber was universally known as "the Phantom"—a term that was thenceforth on everyone's lips, whether its users hailed him as an exemplary hero or damned him as a vile villain whose activities were undermining the very fabric of society.

The only comfort that the gentry and mercantile classes of Teirbrun could find in the midst of their sore distress was to say to one another: "If he persists in his daring depredations, which he shows every sign of doing, then he will surely be caught in the end, one way or another—and then we shall have our revenge. We can certainly rely on Monsieur Sevanter and Jean Funeste to make a fine example of him!"

II.

The names of Alphonse Sevanter and Jean Funeste were very often coupled whenever they were mentioned within the walls of Teirbrun, although they were men of very different quality. They had been friends since boyhood, in spite of the yawning gulf between their social stations.

Alphonse Sevanter's father, Gabriel, claimed that his full surname was Sevanter d'Ys, that he was descended from the mysterious royal family that had founded the town that eventually became the city of Is, and that he was, in fact, the legitimate Duc d'Ys, although the wicked princes who had usurped his position and reduced Is to its present state of degeneracy stubbornly refused to recognize that he had any meaningful title at all. These claims were not taken seriously by anyone in Teirbrun either, but the town's residents were politely sympathetic to the fantasy because it echoed their own delusions of precedence and superiority. Anyone in Teirbrun who suggested that the old man was a suitable candidate for the lunatic asylum in Is—which kindly received all the madmen in Bretagne, and from which few of them ever returned—received short shrift from his neighbors. The old man's madness never worked to the social disadvantage of his son within the town's walls.

The manor-house in which the so-called Duc and his family lived—situated about a league outside the town wall—was certainly suggestive of a glorious ancestry, but the state of extreme disrepair into which it had fallen was incontrovertible evidence of the hard times on which the family had fallen as its generations had been subjected to the process of inexorable exhaustion that saps the virility from oft-inbred aristocratic lines. Alphonse, like his father before him, was an only child, but he had demonstrated a robustness of constitution in infancy that had filled Gabriel Sevanter with the hope that a glorious renascence of the ancient feudal blood might yet be possible. Before Alphonse was five years old, Gabriel became convinced that he was destined to revive and restore the family's fortunes and status. The inevitable result of this conviction was that Alphonse was spoiled by his father and mother alike, many of his whims being granted that wiser parents might have declined. When Alphonse demanded that the son of his father's gardener be allowed to keep company with him, initially as a playmate and later as a fellow pupil of the tutor hired to educate him, his wish had eventually been granted, at no more expense than a sequence of unendurable tantrums.

Alas, Gabriel Sevanter's vague and fantastic hopes were soon dashed when they came into conflict with harsh reality. The self-styled Duc d'Ys had imagined his son going to Is and taking up the apparent life of a dandy, aided by his astonishing good looks, while secretly training in swordsmanship in order to fight his way to a position of power and influence that would ultimately enable him to send all the corrupt merchant princes packing and establish Is as a true jewel among western cities—the capital not merely of Leonais or even all Bretagne, but of Western Christendom entire. Unfortunately, Alphonse did not grow up as handsome as his father hoped, and exhibited no particular talent for dandyism or swordsmanship, but did possess sufficient intelligence to realize that if he were to make any kind of economic or social progress in the world, he would have to acquire a profession.

Fortunately, Alphonse's tutor had been graciously permitted to introduce him to the fundamentals of the law in his youth, and it was a simple matter, once Alphonse decided that he needed to make his own living, to extend that elementary education into an intense and focused training, in order that he might take the requisite examinations in Is and be licensed as a local magistrate. This enterprise proved wholly successful, and Alphonse Sevanter—who never used the supplement to his name to which his father clung so stubbornly, in honor of the sacred but oft-ignored principle that all men are equal before the law—became the first Magistrate of the High Court of Teirbrun when the town was granted such an institution. It was, of course, a great honor for the town to be given that privilege, rather than merely forming part of the circuit followed twice a year by a representative of the Royal Court of Is.

Because Jean Funeste, the gardener's son, received exactly the same education as his childhood friend while continuing to serve as his companion and assistant—although he could not, of course, be entered for any examinations—Monsieur Sevanter the Magistrate had no hesitation in appointing him his clerk. The close association between the two men therefore continued throughout their adulthood, and was always far more than merely professional.

When Alphonse Sevanter decided that he ought to be married, for much the same reasons that he had decided that he ought to have a profession, he begun paying court to the beautiful daughter of one of the town's most wealthiest and most influential citizens, the wine-merchant Paul Mansard. Naturally enough, he made considerable employment of Jean Funeste as an assistant in his suit. On the one hand, the clerk served as a go-between, carrying the formal correspondence conducted between the magistrate and the merchant and the informal correspondence conducted between the magistrate and the merchant's daughter, Blanche. On the other hand, and even more usefully, Funeste accepted the awkward diplomatic task of explaining to the self-styled Duc d'Ys exactly why it made perfect sense for his son to marry the beautiful daughter of a rich merchant rather than the daughter of some worthy nobleman—although he was, of course, far too diplomatic ever to mention that only a nobleman in exceedingly dire circumstances would ever contemplate marrying even his plainest daughter to the son of such a crazy poseur. When the marriage took place, Jean Funeste loyally swore to remain a bachelor for life, in order that he might continue to serve the interests of his master's household without distraction—and he stuck to that resolution, even when Madame Sevanter died, a mere five years later, having borne Monsieur Sevanter one son and three daughters.

The friendship that existed between these two men behind the scenes of public life was, however, universally regarded as the minor and trivial part of their association. What gave rise to the very frequent coupling of their names on the lips of others was their conduct in Teirbrun's court-room, which almost amounted to a theatrical performance. Their long intimacy had given them an ease of mutual understanding and a deftness in their conversation that was extremely rare in the courts of Bretagne.

Whereas most clerks simply wrote down what the law required them to write, while maintaining a dutiful silence, and most magistrates spoke only the formulas specified by protocol, Jean Funeste and Alphonse Sevanter maintained a continual exchange of significant expressions and perceptive remarks. Their dialogue was as full of clever quips as it was of incisive comment. Their exchanges frequently evoked wild laughter in the public gallery of the court, even when the said gallery was packed with the friends of the butt of their jokes. They were capable of demolishing any defense with insidious sarcasm and subtle ridicule. Most of their scathing remarks were, of course, directed at the accused persons brought before them, but the advocates pleading for the accused were by no means immune to their subtle assaults, especially if they were strangers in the town—which they usually were, because the lawyers of Teirbrun became understandably reluctant to represent their neighbors.

To say that there was a certain lightness about his manner of conducting a trial is not to suggest that there was any leniency in Monsieur Sevanter's sentencing. Even in that matter, though, the cleverness and wit of the great man shone through. Skillfully aided by Jean Funeste, Monsieur Sevanter was quite inventive in his choice of punishments, sometimes devising penalties that were previously unheard of in the whole of Bretagne, even though most of the kingdom's subjects believed that the customary scheme of punishment to be perfectly adequate and not inapt. Although it certainly has to be admitted that there is a certain natural justice in the practices of hanging murderers and repeat offenders of every sort, depriving first-offending thieves of a hand, and burning traitors and heretics at the stake, many hearers of this tale will probably agree with Monsieur Sevanter that the simplicity of this scheme is conducive to a certain monotony and tediousness, and that its full deterrent effect is best maintained by occasional ingenious embellishment.

Visitors from Is occasionally opined that Monsieur Sevanter's method of conducting trials was not entirely in accordance with the principle of fairness that was supposed to underlie the law, and that his sentencing was sometimes frankly atrocious. The poorer townsfolk of Teirbrun were inclined to agree with them, but the town's wealthier citizens opposed such opinions fervently. The judgment of the gentry—who were obliged by local pretension to consider the law as a beautiful instrument designed to protect them from the anarchic tendencies of the poor—was that Monsieur Sevanter's sentencing embodied the true spirit of the law far more closely than any pre-ordained scheme of punishment. For his own part, Monsieur Sevanter only said that he did his best to make a punishment fit the crime by which it was earned. For example, a thief apprehended for the first time was often sentenced by Monsieur Sevanter not merely to lose a hand, but also to be branded upon the forehead—with the actual imprint of the object he had stolen, if it were made of metal, or by a sketch drawn with a branding-iron if not—so that he would present his fellow men thereafter with a permanent warning of his covetousness.

In order that this kind of supplementation should not become as monotonous as the customary schedule of punishments, Monsieur Sevanter and Jean Funeste elaborated it considerably as their careers progressed over decades. One man who stole a bolt of fine velvet cloth—an item of great value in civilized Bretagne—not only lost a hand but was condemned to go abroad by day clad in a shirt of prickly hair, which tickled his skin so horribly that it eventually drove him to suicide. A man convicted of poisoning his wife was not only placed in the public pillory for a day, as the written law demanded, but given a series of noxious brews to drink while he was there, so that he was subjected to continual explosive diarrhea—which did not inhibit the usual routine of assaults from behind once dusk fell. He, too, did not long survive the uncomfortable experience.

Even the poorer people of Teirbrun were able to perceive an exquisite intelligence at work in these augmented punishments, and the loyal public who flocked to see the public executioner at work thought Alphonse Sevanter and Jean Funeste a pair of fine fellows. Monsieur Sevanter was therefore a very popular man in the town, frequently called "the Great Judge." Even the Phantom's most avid admirers could not help wondering what ingeniously amusing indignities the Great Judge would inflict upon the burglar when he was finally caught, before he was hanged and left to rot upon the gibbet. The Phantom's afflictions occurred in the twenty-fifth year of Monsieur Sevanter's magistracy, when the Great Judge was at the pinnacle of his fame.

III.

The so-called Phantom been at his work for some time before anyone noticed that a strange pattern was becoming discernible within the elaborate sequence of his more recent crimes.

Paul Mansard's wife had long hosted a soirée once a week for family friends, at which Alphonse Sevanter was an invariable guest—the only fixture at the table who was not a merchant. Every guest had his allotted seat at the table, and the arrangement never varied; whenever one of the merchants was away on business, his seat remained empty. Monsieur Sevanter, as Mansard's son-in-law, had the seat to the host's right. It was not surprising that the regulars at this soirée were numbered among the Phantom's victims, as they were among the most prosperous of the town's citizens, but it did seem surprising, once the fact was noticed and pointed out, that they were targeted in order of the seating plan, starting at the lower end of the table, alternating between the left and right and working gradually towards its head.

The Phantom did not, of course, restrict himself to plundering the guests at Madame Mansard's table, and it was rare for two of the attendees to be robbed one after another; there were unusually two or three robberies in between those afflicting the soirée's population. Even so, it eventually became apparent that that once a particular person at the table had been robbed, the next person in the seating sequence would be victimized before any of the other guests.

When this pattern was noticed, the discovery seemed fortunate, for it indicated a possible means of predicting the Phantom's predations. As each guest's turn arrived, he would borrow extra watchmen and alert the constables, who would often lie in wait for days on end, waiting for the anticipated raid. The first effect of this practice was, however, that the people unconnected with Madame Mansard's soirées who were robbed in the interim began to protest that they had been deprived of protection, and that the favor given to Mansard's friends was making it easier for the robber to victimize them. The fact that the extra protection given to the anticipated victims never prevented the Phantom from gaining access to their homes and making off with his chosen loot did not lessen this resentment.

As the fundamental pattern advanced, drawing ever nearer to the head of Paul Mansard's table, another peculiarity began to manifest itself in the Phantom's other raids. A number of burglaries occurred in which no objects of real value were removed, but only single items whose value was chiefly sentimental. All these burglaries took place at the houses of Monsieur Sevanter's relatives: one at his father's old manor house—where the self-styled Duc, long widowed and approaching his eightieth year, now lived with a handful of ancient retainers—and the other four at the homes of his children.

Monsieur Sevanter's son and two older daughters had all married tolerably well, but the youngest daughter had been banished from his house in disgrace when she had fallen in love with a young portrait-painter. The portrait-painter's house was the second of the five to be burgled, after the Duc's, and was by far the poorest of all those so far raided by the Phantom; it was hardly surprising that he had found no coin or jewels in such a place to steal, although it seemed distinctly odd that he should bother to steal a carved wooden heart, which had been given to the painter's wife by the mother she had lost in infancy. This became less astonishing in retrospect, though, when he took similar trinkets from the houses of Monsieur Sevanter's other three children, ignoring objects of more manifest value and not even bothering to search for hidden coin. It was quite obvious that the Phantom was deliberately targeting the relatives of the Great Judge, not for personal gain, but merely, it seemed, in order to taunt and insult him.

When the news of this new departure in the Phantom's procedure spread through the town, the general opinion was that the Phantom must be engaged in exacting revenge upon Alphonse Sevanter for some indignity inflicted upon him in the Great Judge's court. Everyone in the neighborhood who had ever appeared before Monsieur Sevanter and had lived to tell the tale immediately became the object of curious speculation. Amazingly, even having discounted all those who only had one hand, there were more than a hundred; twenty-five years is a long time. Most of those who attracted attention in this way hastened to provide alibis for as many as possible of the nights when the Phantom had perpetrated his crimes, but a few actually enjoyed the notoriety and were eager to make sure that their vehement denials had a hint of irony about them.

Following this short series of exceptional, and seemingly-personal, burglaries, all the town's law-enforcement agents began to concentrate their efforts of Monsieur Sevanter's own house. Not only did he seem to be the next likely victim in that sequence, but it was also his turn to be robbed by virtue of his position at Paul Mansard's dinner-table; all the other guests had already fallen victim to the Phantom, except for Paul Mansard himself, whose position at its head entitled him to be the last in the sequence.

Monsieur Sevanter was, by now, extremely annoyed with the Phantom. Although even his faithful and devoted friend Jean Funeste would never have described him as a loving man, he had a very strong sense of family. He had been very careful not to spoil his own children in the manner that he had been spoiled by his parents, because the last thing in the world he wanted was to be subjected in his turn to the kind of tantrums to which he had subjected them, but he was nevertheless very aware of the responsibilities of fatherhood. Why else would he have been so annoyed about the fact that his youngest daughter had married for love? Even though he had not spoken to his daughter for more than a year, he was moved to wrath when he heard of the theft of the wooden heart, and when the robberies at his other children's homes made it appear that the Phantom was teasing him, that wrath became very bitter indeed.

Unwilling merely to wait for the anticipated raid on his own home, Alphonse Sevanter let it be known through the town that he would personally double the price that the mayor had already been persuaded to place on the robber's head, so that the men who caught the rogue would have a thousand silver sequins to divide between them. No reward of that dimension had ever been offered in Teirbrun for the apprehension of a felon, and the sum was quoted with avaricious wonderment in the town's meaner streets. Every honest beggar and as-yet-unapprehended thief began to watch his friends with avaricious care, and every unhappy child yearned to discover proof that one or other of his parents might prove to be the burglar, and thus exchangeable for ready money—but when none of the poor could find the Phantom among his acquaintances, the rumor began to be put about that the robber must be a gentleman.

The opinion that the Phantom might be a gentleman was given further credence when the burglar was very nearly apprehended in the garden of a pork-butcher from whom he had just stolen a bag of silver and a pair of brand-new dueling-pistols, of a sort that had only recently come on to the market in Bretagne. This time, the man who tried to stop him was no nightshirted milksop but a burly watchman named Hernand, armed with a halberd. The watchman engaged the masked thief with alacrity, the pressure of his duty reinforced by greed.

Hernand thrust at the Phantom as cunningly as he knew how, but his halberd was a rather cumbersome weapon and his opponent somehow contrived to parry every blow with his own much smaller weapon.

"Three times I drove him to the wall," the watchman declared, when he gave an account of his adventure to the mayor, Paul Mansard, Odo and Monsieur Sevanter, "and thrice he slipped away, as delicately as if he were dancing. I could not see his face, but I know now that he is a well-schooled fencer, who fights as only a light-footed sportsman fights, and very cleverly. Although he dresses himself in the plainest leather when he undertakes his larcenies, I would wager everything I have that he is used to calfskin and lace!"

"Did the wretch speak to you at all?" demanded Monsieur Sevanter, who found this ration of information far too meager to assuage his hunger for news.

"Yes, he did," Hernand admitted. "When he finally tripped me up and took my halberd away, he said that he was sorry to have put me to the inconvenience of chasing him, but that he could not be caught until he had settled his account with the so-called Great Judge which he hoped to do within the week. I did not recognize his voice, alas!"

When Monsieur Sevanter heard of this amazing insolence his hands literally shook with wrath, and he had to ask Jean Funeste—who was well-used to taking dictation from him—to write down a proclamation for him, which he then gave to the Town Crier, demanding that it be loudly read in every quarter of the town.

The message that the crier gave out was this:

"I, Alphonse Sevanter, Magistrate of Teirbrun, am sorely annoyed by the miseries inflicted upon my friends and my children by that low felon whom the silly common folk have named the Phantom. I declare that this so-called Phantom is in reality worthy of no name save that of Rascal and Coward, and I say to him that if he bears any grudge against me, then he ought now to direct his attentions to my own house, and to no other. Should he care to answer this challenge, I promise him that he will be caught, exposed for the shabby trickster that he is, and delivered to the kind of justice that his horrid crimes deserve."

This was an unprecedented event. Never before had a magistrate of any town in Bretagne sent such a message in such a fashion. Whether the man for whom it was intended heard it declaimed by the crier, no one could be sure, but wherever it was broadcast there were hundreds of interested ears to catch it and thousands of clucking tongues to pass it on—with the inevitable result that, when the curfew tolled that day, there was no one within the town wall or a three leagues around who had not heard it repeated. The fateful words had been shouted at the eardrums of ancients so deaf they could hardly hear them, and burbled at youngsters so small they could barely understand them, and there was no doubt at all that if the Phantom was anywhere near the town that day, the challenge must have been delivered. The citizens waited, thrilled by excitement, to see what would happen next.

IV.

In the meantime, Monsieur Sevanter had not been idle. Even in the normal course of affairs there was always a militiaman on duty outside his front gate, and another at the rear. He obtained six more from the mayor, in order that the perimeter of his grounds might be regularly patrolled by two pairs of armed guards, working in shifts. He posted watchmen within the surrounding wall, who similarly worked in shifts, four being on duty at all times. The positions these sentries took up, and the numerous lanterns hung from hooks on the outer wall of the house, ensured that there was not a single shadowed covert available to a stealthy intruder.

Within the house Monsieur Sevanter had a staff of thirteen domestics in residence, including six men. Not one of the six was frail, and three of them—the coachman, the groom and his personal valet—were powerful fellows that no intruder would be eager to fight. Monsieur Sevanter ordered that no more than two of these men should be asleep at any time, and that the others should all go armed; to those who were practiced he gave short swords, while those who were unskilled were instructed to carry cudgels.

In addition to these faithful servants, the worthy Jean Funeste also lived in the house as a sort of permanent guest. Although he normally slept in a tiny attic, the clerk declared that he would henceforth sleep in a hammock strung across the outer face of Monsieur Sevanter's bedroom door, so that no one would be able to enter without waking him, and that he would keep a pistol about his person at all times. He showed his friend a pair of dueling-pistols of the very latest model, and insisted that Monsieur Sevanter should keep the second member of the pair himself, hidden under the pillows of his capacious bed.

Nor did Jean Funeste stop at such ordinary precautions as these. Mindful of the possibility that the Phantom's elusiveness might be the result of magic, he offered the use of his own attic room to an astrologer named Furalor, who had as good a reputation for casting defensive spells as he had for predicting the future, even though he was not recognized by the church as an authority on magic. The principal guest-room was made up for Odo, the Archbishop's investigator, in the hope that some evidence might materialize that would justify the summoning of an official witchfinder. Furalor assured Monsieur Sevanter that he would deploy his very best protective measures, setting magical alarms upon the all the doorways and windows, which would make the entire house into a cunning trap, while Odo told the magistrate that he would be very careful to include him in his specific prayers.

Jean Funeste also suggested that Monsieur Sevanter should gather his most precious possessions—especially those that the Phantom might imagine to have sentimental value—into three strong chests fitted with ingenious locks, which should be placed in a locked cupboard in the magistrate's bedroom. The clerk spent an entire evening closeted with his friend, compiling an inventory as the things were put away. The key to the cupboard was placed under Monsieur Sevanter's pillow, along with the pistol, while Jean Funeste kept the keys to the three chests on his person.

Monsieur Sevanter declared himself very satisfied with all these precautions, although he also expressed the opinion that he might perhaps have made his house so utterly impregnable that the Phantom would not even dare try to get into it.

"There are, after all, plenty of houses left in Teirbrun that he has not yet visited," the Great Judge observed, "and it would not be the first time that he has exploited our anticipations as a distraction."

"I suppose a few more greengrocers, fish-factors and candle-makers might suffer at his hands before he plucks up the courage to respond to your challenge" Jean Funeste admitted, "but he has shown every sign of having become addicted to his work. One day—sooner rather than later, I suspect—he will decide that the time has come to risk all our precautions, and will finally bite off more than he can chew. Then, we shall punish him very thoroughly for his impetuousness."

That night, Monsieur Sevanter went to his bed fully determined to sleep as soundly as he normally did, in order to demonstrate his contempt for the Phantom and his faith in the precautions that he had taken. Unfortunately, his composure was not quite adequate to this intention, and he lay tossing and turning for several hours.

Whenever he dozed off briefly, the magistrate found himself beset by horrid nightmares in which men he had sentenced to unusual fatal punishments rose from their paupers' graves to march through the empty streets, heading for an appointed rendezvous with him, which he felt that he would somehow be obliged to keep, whether it might be in the graveyard, a church or the lunatic asylum in Is.

The fourth or fifth time that a bad dream sent him urgently back to wakefulness he felt such an overwhelming impression of dread that he reached for the fire-cord that he had laid beside the bed, ready for an emergency. Having blown vigorously upon it to make it glow brightly he applied it to the tallow nightlight that was nearby.

As soon as the flame caught, he took up the nightlight, holding it before him so that its faint radiance spread as far as it could into the four corners of the room. He did this to reassure himself that he was still alone and safe, but the plan misfired.

He was not alone.

Nor, he felt, as his heart seemed to sink into his belly, was he safe.

Seated at the foot of the bed was a very curious individual. Monsieur Sevanter could not tell whether it was man or woman, not merely because the light shed by the tallow candle was so very meager but because the figure seemed almost to be made of shadow itself. A dark hood concealed the cut of the person's hair, a black cloak depended shapelessly over the contours of the body and a black silk mask hid the upper part of the face. There was no doubt in the magistrate's mind that he was confronted by the infamous Phantom of Teirbrun.

Sevanter opened his mouth to shout for help, but the figure put a slender finger to the lips of its unsmiling mask. The gesture seemed more conspiratorial than threatening, and the magistrate was very well aware of the absurdity of keeping silent, but he nevertheless stifled his call. "How on Earth did you get in here?" he asked, instead, his voice hardly above a whisper.

"Did you really think that you could keep me out?" asked the visitor. The voice was light, but had an odd throaty quality. Monsieur Sevanter could not tell whether it was man's or woman's. "My magic is far more powerful than your petty precautions."

"Magic?" the magistrate echoed. "Do you confess, then, to being a witch, in league with the Devil?"

"There is more magic in the world that that bestowed by the Devil," the Phantom retorted, "and better magic too."

Privately, Alphonse Sevanter had never believed in the power of magic, and had always thought witchfinders as fraudulent in their dealings as charlatans like Furalor, but it was not an opinion he had ever dared express openly, even to Jean Funeste—although he had always suspected that Funeste's apparent belief in magic and the power of the Church to resist it was as much a pretence as his own. He had only attempted to solicit a confession of witchcraft in the hope of putting some vigor into Odo's rather listless "investigation".

"Did Hernand not tell you that I would come to you within the week, Great Judge?" the Phantom continued, when Monsieur Sevanter made no reply to his last remark. "Did you doubt that I meant what I said? Was it not, therefore, rather silly as well as unnecessary to issue so public an invitation?"

"What do you want with me, thief?" asked Monsieur Sevanter, his own voice grating a little because his mouth was so dry.

"Only justice," said the other, "and a punishment to fit your crime. I came tonight simply to pass sentence upon you—you must wait, as I have long waited, for the sentence to be carried out. I shall return again tomorrow to hear your plea for mercy...and on the third night, the sentence will take effect."

"What sentence?" whispered Monsieur Sevanter, feeling an urgent wish to know what the Phantom planned.

"No ordinary fate," said the voice from behind the mask. "Like yourself, I am not so lenient." The figure moved then, perhaps extending an arm, but the light was too poor to allow Monsieur Sevanter to be sure—until there was a sudden explosion of brilliant white light, of the kind projected by naval flares. The magistrate's dark-adjusted eyes were immediately overwhelmed by the flood of light, and he was blinded

Then, and only then, did the magistrate panic. He let loose a long scream whose echoes must have extended into every corridor and alcove in the house. As he screamed, some reflex made him raise his arms and place his hands in front of his face, as if to protect himself from an attack—but no attack came. When a seeming eternity had passed—although it was presumably no more than a few seconds—he dropped his arm again and blinked furiously, trying to recover the power of vision.

He had just enough time to see that the room seemed quite empty before the door was thrown back on its hinges, and Jean Funeste rushed in, clad in a capacious dark blue nightshirt and an absurd matching night-cap. The clerk was, however, brandishing a pistol in his left hand and a full three feet of polished blade in his right, ready to thrust or slash. At exactly the same moment, Furalor's voice was heard emerging from the stairs to the attic, crying: "The alarm is triggered! The alarm is triggered! The judge's door has been breached by magic!"

Within minutes the footman and the coachman arrived, then the yawning Odo, and finally the other weary servants, one after another, blades and cudgels at the ready. There was nothing for them to do, alas. There was no one in the room but Alphonse Sevanter, sitting up in bed and looking rather foolish, his pale face scrubbed clean of powder and paint. Servants were quickly sent to interrogate the watchmen, but they had seen no one enter the house and no one leave.

The room offered no obvious hiding places, except for the locked cupboard, but it was searched with absurd thoroughness. When the cupboard was unlocked, the three chests were found to be still inside, all securely locked. In the meantime, encouraged by Jean Funeste and Odo, Monsieur Sevanter gave a full and detailed account of his conversation with the Phantom. The clerk wrote it all down, in order that a copy might be sent to the mayor, and carefully ascertained that no detail was omitted. Even the substance of Monsieur Sevanter's nightmares was recorded, along with the suggestive enquiry regarding witchcraft and its reply—which Odo, unsurprisingly, refused to accept as final proof that diabolism or heresy had played any part in the episode.

Furalor swore by the entire zodiac that no one could have passed through the magically-alarmed door before the alarm was raised. The militiamen patrolling the perimeter were summoned, and they too testified that no one could possibly have clambered over the wall without being seen. The watchmen were questioned again, more formally, and repeated their confident assertion that no one could possibly have reached any of the doors, or clambered up to any of the shuttered window—whose shutters were still closed tight—without being seen.

On considering these facts, everyone except Monsieur Sevanter eventually came to the conclusion that no one had entered the room at all, and that the magistrate must have dreamed his encounter with the Phantom, as a continuation of his earlier sequence of nightmares.

In order to save the magistrate's feelings, however, his servants assured him that he must have been the victim of a magic spell, which had compelled him to see someone who was not physically present.

Although he had his own private doubts by now, the magistrate did not like to think that such panic had been aroused in him by a mere illusion, and he continued to insist that the Phantom really had been there. Furalor muttered darkly about the possible involvement of a more robust kind of magic, but Odo hastened to assure the astrologer that the black magicians of Bretagne, numerous as they might be, were incapable of flying through the air, walking through walls and vanishing into thin air. The monk's expert opinion was that, if any magic at all had been involved, it could only have been of the suggestive sort mentioned by the servants.

Unfortunately, the conclusion that Monsieur Sevanter had only dreamed his encounter with the Phantom, or had been deluded into imagining it by some subtle spell, came to seem slightly less probable later that morning, when he and Jean Funeste decided to make another inventory of the three chests of valuables, in order to make sure that nothing was missing. Although none of the locks—including the lock on the cupboard door—appeared to have been forced, a single item appeared to have been removed from each of the chests. Each of the objects was far from being the most valuable in its respective strongbox, the most costly of them all being a silver comb, with which the Madame Sevanter had often used to put up her lovely hair, but the fact of their theft was indubitable.

"There is a pattern here, Jean," Monsieur Sevanter immediately said to his friend. "All three objects belonged to my late wife; in addition to the comb, the enameled brooch and the lacquered fan were also hers, as you very probably remember. My father, my children, my long-dead wife…it's as if the Phantom were weaving an intricate web around me, approaching me with all possible indirection while refusing to attack me directly. What can it all mean?"

"I hardly know what to say," Jean Funeste replied. "It is a profound mystery."

Monsieur Sevanter swore all those involved in the affair to the utmost secrecy regarding the details of the raid—with the inevitable result that every single item was all around the town by noon, being earnestly studied and discussed by beldames and bakers, school-teachers and soldiers, and even road-sweepers and ragamuffins.

V.

There is only one thing that the poor people of a town love more than a heroic villain, and that is a mystery. The citizens of Teirbrun traded questions with avid interest. The mere matter of the Phantom's identity faded into the background, largely displaced by more exotic matters of concern. What black magic or ingenious trickery had allowed the burglar to enter the magistrate's house and escape again undetected? Why had he told the magistrate that he would return twice more, and then gone away without attempting to hurt him? How and why had he taken the silver comb and other carefully locked-up objects belonging to the long-dead Madame Sevanter? All these puzzles received careful consideration, but none of course could compare in fascination with the most intriguing question of all. What sentence had been passed on Teirbrun's Great Judge? What punishment, to fit what crime?

The common people racked their memories once again to recall every criminal on whom Monsieur Sevanter had ever passed sentence, living or dead. The scrutiny to which the surviving victims of Monsieur Sevanter's justice had already been subject was expanded to include the children of those who had not survived it. "What other significance can possibly be attached to the targeting of Monsieur Sevanter's family?" the street-corner philosophers asked one another. "This is no more matter of violent revenge; the person who is doing this must have had his life blighted by the removal of someone beloved."

The rumor spread like wildfire that some unlucky person singled out by the Great Judge for a particularly nasty punishment must in fact have been innocent of his crime, and that the bloody libel of his false conviction, whose burden had fallen upon his entirely family, was finally about to be wiped out, and the penalty repaid in full measure, not merely by the magistrate himself but by all the magistrate's relatives and friends. Alphonse Sevanter did not stir from his house that day, but that did not prevent him from hearing the cries and cheers of the ragged and hungry children of the street, several of whom informed him with delighted squeals that he was doomed, and that the second morrow thereafter would be the most miserable of his whole existence.

The humble people of Teirbrun were not the only ones who were struggling to recall some particular case that might give a clue to the Phantom's identity. Paul Mansard—the only member of his wife's dining-club who had not yet been robbed—was very anxious to avoid that eventuality, and he demanded that the mayor call an extraordinary meeting of the Town Council to discuss the "crisis".

Monsieur Sevanter was as determined as anyone to find the vital clue that might lead to the Phantom's identification and arrest, and he demanded that Jean Funeste fetch the court records and read them aloud to him while he listened with closed eyes and cast his mind back, trying to convert the scrupulously-compiled lists of indictments into the images faces and voices, and trying desperately to obtain some intuition therefrom.

The loyal clerk did as he was asked, for hours on end. Monsieur Sevanter told him to pause several times—when he mentioned three highway thieves whose feet he had ordered flayed, so that they might never walk the roads again; when he named two prostitutes convicted of picking their clients' pockets, whose own "pockets" the magistrate had ordered to be sown up tightly with catgut; when he pronounced the names of a tax-evader who had been castrated in order to remind them of the condition that the town would be in if adequate provision were not to be made for its defense against marauders—but none of the chords struck by those names resonated sufficiently to persuade the magistrate that they held the key.

"All those were relatively trivial matters," Monsieur Sevanter opined, with a sigh, when Funeste was only a tenth of the way through the list. "All things considered, the only kind of case likely to have evoked such an extraordinary response as the Phantom's is a case of murder. From now on, only read out the names of individuals convinced of murder."

Funeste continued enumerating the murderers condemned to death by Monsieur Sevanter, who eventually turned out to number two hundred and fifty-two—barely one a month, averaged over their long tenure. In the main, it was a conspicuously tedious list. The additional cleverness with which the deaths of some of the accused had been contrived had usually added little enough suffering to the ordeals prescribed by the law. There seemed to be no one on the list who had not fully merited death, and no one whose family had any good reason to take particular umbrage.

Monsieur Sevanter then decided that they ought to concentrate their attention on people who had committed crimes allegedly involving magic—for he was increasingly sure in his own mind that the Phantom's references to magic must hold some significance, even if no material magic could have been involved in the remarkable events of the night. Alas, Jean Funeste did not need to consult the records closely in order to remind Monsieur Sevanter that he had never had occasion to pass sentence on an authentic wizard, or even a witch who could be convincingly asserted to have been a regular attendee at the Devil's sabbats. If such a person had ever committed crimes in Teirbrun, he or she had not been apprehended—a fact which, on reflection, could hardly be deemed surprising.

In the previous twenty-five years, a rapid survey of the unread names ascertained, the ever-vigilant watchmen and constables—aided and abetted by the Church's agents—had contrived to arrest thirteen practitioners of unorthodox medicine, half a dozen confidence tricksters posing as alchemists and four hagwives accused of trivial spell-casting. The most dangerous of the lot had been one of the herbalists, whose potions had turned out to be mildly poisonous—but one could say the same about half the town's licensed physicians. In any case, his punishment had been relatively mild and not particularly unusual—he had been buried in the earth up to his neck and subjected to a shower of dung and small stones hurled in an entirely unmagical fashion by his victims, which had driven him mad and resulted in his incarceration in the notorious lunatic asylum of Is, from which he had never returned.

"Perhaps we are overlooking the obvious," Monsieur Sevanter said, with a sight. "The Phantom is, after all, a thief—but thieves constitute the vast majority of names on the list."

"And almost all of them suffered the commonplace penalties of losing a hand and carrying a brand," Funeste observed. "Fates that are unlikely to generate any particular animosity even in the most devoted brother or son."

"He is, moreover, as *master* thief," Monsieur Sevanter went on, ignoring the interjection. "There are, I dare say, schools of larceny in Is—universities of larceny, even—whose students are thoroughly schooled in the arts of stealth, lock-picking and the like as well as the use of weapons, but there is nothing in our records to tell us whether any dispossessed sons of Teirbrun might have attended such schools in the recent or distant past."

"On the whole," said Jean Funeste, "I think it unlikely. Having been privileged to share your own education—without, alas, the advantage of your superior intelligence—I know how direly difficult it is for a common man to acquire expertise in any art. This Phantom must have worked extremely hard to educate himself, if he is not, as some rumor-mongers allege, a gentleman."

"There's not a gentleman in town who has not suffered at his hands," Monsieur Sevanter said, intemperately.

"It's not impossible that the Phantom might have robbed his own house by way of distraction," Jean Funeste suggested. "And your generalization is not quite correct. There is one man who has not yet been targeted—the richest of them all, if rumor can be believed."

"Paul Mansard," the magistrate said, taking the inference without difficulty. "But he has suffered while I have suffered, for my children are his grandchildren. It's absurd even to think that he would have offended the guests at his own table, ticking them off his carefully-ordered list one by one."

"Of course it is," Jean Funeste agreed. "He is busy as we speak trying to rouse the mayor to more urgent action—and I believe that he is quite ready to assume mayoral office himself if necessary. He is a man of action, and I dare say that he would exercise municipal authority in the manner of a true merchant prince, the equal of any in Is."

"Idle chatter is not helping us," Monsieur Sevanter reminded him. "Forget my father-in-law and focus on my persecutor."

The clerk obeyed—but it was all to no avail.

Their utter failure to find any inspiration in the court lists only served to redouble Monsieur Sevanter's determination to protect himself from the second promised visit of the Phantom. The permanently-patrolling guard outside the house was increased to eight, and the number of stationary watchmen inside the grounds was similarly doubled. All of the servants, trained or not, were issued with blades.

Jean Funeste re-checked both the dueling-pistols to make certain that they were properly loaded, and that the firing-mechanisms were in good working order. He suggested to his friend that there was no point in holding further conversations with the burglar, and that the magistrate should simply shoot the villain down like a dog. Monsieur Sevanter agreed that this was the only course of action likely to be effective were the Phantom to succeed, against all the odds, in gaining entry to his bedroom again. In order to leave no possible precaution in a state neglect, however, he permitted Funeste to ask Furalor to reinforce his alarm spells and to implore Odo to increase the urgency of his prayers.

Again, Jean Funeste placed himself immediately outside the magistrate's unlocked bedroom door, as a final line of external defense. He added an extra padlock to the door of the cupboard where the treasure-chests were stored, and hid the key very carefully in a cranny between the bedroom's floorboards, keeping that depository secret from everyone except himself and Monsieur Sevanter.

When darkness came, Monsieur Sevanter made no attempt to go to sleep, having resolved this time to remain awake. He kept no less than five wax candles burning in his room. Alas, as the night wore on, his determination to stay alert was put to an increasingly severe test by a seductive drowsiness that continually crept up on him.

Four or five times the magistrate drifted off to sleep, only to dream each time that all the men he had ever condemned to death were rising from their graves and marching through the streets of Teirbrun, calling out to him to meet them at a place assigned by destiny, to which he *knew* that he would in time be drawn—and this time, he was certain that the meeting would not be in a graveyard or a church, although he could not quite determine exactly where it would take pace.

No sooner had Monsieur Sevanter lost count of the occasions on which this happened than he opened his eyes with a sudden start, and realized that all but one of the candles had gone out, perhaps deliberately extinguished. By the light of the one remaining candle he saw a vague figure standing at the foot of the bed, seemingly wrapped around by a dark cloak. Shadowed eyes were staring at him through two almond-shaped holes cut in a mask.

"It will do no good to strive against your fate, Magistrate," said a voice, which sounded like the rustling of fallen leaves stirred by a cold north wind. "Sentence has already been passed, and only remains to be carried out."

This time, Monsieur Sevanter did not pause to debate matters with the Phantom. Nor did he bother to cry out to rouse his many friends and protectors. Instead, he reached under his pillow, brought out the pistol, took rapid aim and fired.

The effect of what he did was not quite what he had expected. Instead of an instant explosion there was a sinister hiss and a huge gout of white smoke, which stung his eyes horribly, blinding him. The detonation was delayed for what seemed like an eternity, although it was probably no more than half a second. The pistol's recoil wrenched his fingers and his wrist quite painfully, causing him to drop the weapon. Monsieur Sevanter screamed for help, rubbing his eyes furiously

When the smoke had finally cleared and he had contrived to remove the tears from his eyes, the magistrate was not at all surprised to find that the visitor was no longer standing at the foot of his bed. He threw back his sheets and leapt to the floor, hoping—if not actually expecting—to find the Phantom lying full length on the floor, with a gaping hole in his breast, covered in blood.

Alas, there was no corpse on his carpet.

The door opened to admit the sword-wielding and pistol-brandishing Funeste, dressed in the same blue cap-and-gown as the previous night, followed by a veritable army of armed warriors. Monsieur Sevanter stamped his feet like a madman and howled with rage and frustration. Furalor's voice could be heard in the attic, screeching: "The alarms! The alarms! The door is breached, and so are the chests!"

The servants made another dutiful search, but it was quite obvious that they did not expect to find anything. They did not seem at all surprised that no sign of the Phantom's presence remained.

"But I shot him!" Monsieur Sevanter protested, feebly. "I shot him in the heart!"

"Alas," said Jean Funeste, pointing to one of the dark-stained wooden panels in which the wall opposite the bed was clad, "The bullet is here, embedded in the wall. Had the Phantom really been standing at the foot of your bed, it would indeed have struck him in the heart—but it seems to have passed clean through him."

"Do you doubt me, Jean?" the magistrate cried. "Are you telling me that he was not really here, and that I have been dreaming?"

"No, of course not!" the clerk hastened to reassure him. "If you say that he was here, in the flesh, then I believe with all my heart that he was here. He must have ducked as you fired, and the bullet must have passed over his head."

"The trigger did not act immediately!" Monsieur Sevanter was quick to say. "There was a slight delay—no more than half a second, I dare say, but probably time enough to allow a man with lightning reflexes to duck!"

"I shall clean and repair the firing-mechanism with the utmost care," the clerk promised, "and I shall make absolutely certain that there is no delay the next time the weapon is fired—but I wonder how the Phantom could possibly have made his exit after ducking, for I would swear that no more than half a second more elapsed between my hearing the shot and bursting through that door."

"Well," said the magistrate, "there is one way to be certain as whether he was here or not. We must examine the chests, to see whether anything has been stolen."

"We ought to make a record first," Jean Funeste said, "While all the details are fresh in your memory. There might be some detail therein that will permit us to get to the bottom of the mystery."

Alas, even when the most scrupulous record of the evening's events had been compiled, it was impossible to detect any detail therein that might offer a clue of the Phantom's identity or *modus operandi*.

When the servants had all been dismissed from their presence, Jean Funeste recovered the key to the padlock from its hiding-place, and then took the key to the cupboard door from under the magistrate's pillow. Through the rest of the night, Monsieur Sevanter and his clerk worked methodically through their inventory. By the time dawn came, they were certain that one thing—and one thing only—had been removed from each of the three chests. The most valuable of these items was a fine embroidered chemise, trimmed with the fur of a rare white hare, which the long-dead Madame Sevanter had employed as her favorite nightshirt. The other two objects had also belonged to her. Both men wore sorrowful expressions as they locked the chests again and replaced them in the cupboard, before Jean Funeste went to attend to his other duties and fulfill his other promises

Monsieur Sevanter did not trouble to swear his domestics to secrecy again, for he knew by now how futile such gesture would be. The whole town seemed to know what had happened almost before the rising sun was clear of the horizon, and by noon there was not a single detail of the night's events that had escaped the scrupulous attention of the gossips.

VI.

When he had eaten a far-from-hearty mid-day meal the magistrate summoned Jean Funeste, Odo and Furalor to a conference. He implored all three to help him make some sense out of what had happened. In his desperation, he even begged Furalor to tell him what kind of magic might have been worked to bring the Phantom into his room despite all possible precautions, and to leave it again so cleverly.

"Well," said the astrologer, who had been racking his brains for some time in the hope of excusing the failure of his magical alarms to wake him until after the event they were supposed to anticipate, "it seems to me that we can only conclude that the so-called Phantom is indeed a phantom, in a perfectly literal sense. He cannot be an ordinary man protected by some kind of spell or potion of invisibility, for he does not come through the door or the window. He can only be a ghost—and since his efforts appear, in the ultimate analysis, to be focused on this house, he is probably the ghost of someone who died in this house."

"A ghost!" exclaimed Monsieur Sevanter, who had not previously given any serious thought to the possibility that the Phantom might really be a phantom, but was now sufficiently desperate to leave no potentially-comforting straw unclutched. "Whose ghost?"

Furalor hesitated, seemingly reluctant to pronounce the name he had in mind. "I am truly sorry, Monsieur, to voice what may seem to be a shocking thought," he eventually said, "but I believe that we must consider your late wife the most likely candidate."

"My late wife, you star-struck imbecile!" exclaimed the magistrate, causing Furalor to recoil in apparent horror. "If that's what passes for divination in your idiot profession, then it's even more useless than I've long believed. My wife has been dead for twenty years. All our children are married, and two have children of their own. If my late wife wanted to haunt me—and I certainly never did her any wrong—why has she been idle these last twenty years?"

Furalor appeared to be making a considerable effort to suppress his resentment at the brutal dismissal of his suggestion and the casual insult to his vocation. "I merely took note, sir," he said, as mildly as he could "of that fact that the things that the Phantom has taken from you appear to be things that your wife once owned. Can you remember, perchance, whether it was your wife who gave to your other children the things that were subsequently removed from their possession?"

While the astrologer was speaking, a deep scowl had taken possession of the magistrate's face, but Monsieur Sevanter suppressed his anger. He was a man used to weighing evidence and drawing scrupulous conclusions—and when he considered the question that Furalor had posed, he realized that all the objects removed from the houses of his son and daughters had indeed been given to them by their mother. Even the trinket stolen from his father's house had been a birthday gift from her.

"But what possible reason could my late wife have for haunting me?" complained the magistrate. "I was as just and fair in my dealings with her as I am with the world at large. She lived and died in comfort, with all that a woman could desire. She had the privilege of bearing four fine children, and would have borne five had she not had the misfortune to die in the final attempt. I cannot believe that she might want to hurt me."

"And yet," Odo put in, apparently more sympathetic to the astrologer's hypothesis than might have been expected, given that his master the Archbishop presumably had not wanted him to discover any need for the services of an exorcist, any more than he had wanted him to find any need for the dispatch of a witchfinder, "there is surely other evidence to incline us in the direction of an explanation of this kind. You have admitted that each time you have seen the Phantom, you have awakened momentarily from a dream in which graves seemed to open to yield up their dead, and that you have had a sense of being drawn to some fateful rendezvous. Perhaps your encounters with the Phantom *were* the meetings of which your dreams spoke. Perhaps you are indeed being harassed by an unquiet spirit—whether at the Devil's instigation or with the Lord's permission I cannot tell."

"No doubt it was kind of the Lord to send me an illuminating vision," said Monsieur Sevanter, with an offensive sharpness that was suggestive of tacit atheism as well as gross rudeness, "but I wish that he had taken the trouble to make it a little more explicit."

At this, the monk shook his head, trying to pretend that the gesture was motivated by sorrow rather than resentment. "We are the servants of the Lord," he said. "He is not ours. We should be grateful for any enlightenment He might send, not resentful that He has not told us more."

"Very true," said Furalor, piously. "The stars in God's firmament undoubtedly give us information, but never clearly; we must be grateful for what we can deduce, rather than complaining that horoscopes do not speak to us with a peasant's bluntness or a scholar's precision."

Monsieur Sevanter's scowl deepened even further, and he turned to his closest friend. "This is all nonsense, Jean, is it not?" he said. "Assure me, please, that there is another way of interpreting this case, which these silly men have overlooked."

"Well," said Jean Funeste, smoothly, "it certainly seems to me that there are several facts that are difficult to explain within Monsieur Furalor's theory. The Phantom has certainly not been restricted to the bounds of this house, as haunters are traditionally supposed to be. He has not confined his attentions to the houses of Monsieur Sevanter's kin. He has carried out raids all over Teirbrun, many of them purely for profit, and he has often carried away very substantial bundles of loot. He was certainly solid enough to slice the buttons from a grocer's nightshirt and to engage the watchman Hernand in a material clash of arms. I cannot imagine for a moment that such actions could have been those of the late Madame Sevanter, who was a rather frail woman and very gentle of temperament."

"Quite so!" cried the magistrate. "What have you to say to that, Master Astrologer? Since the magical alarms you placed on my treasure-chests have proved so ineffective, we can hardly be sure that the others you have set were not equally defective. It is my firm belief that this Phantom is as solid as you and me, although he would not have to be much of a magician for your silly little spells to be utterly impotent to keep him at bay!"

"Well," replied Furalor, in the offended tone that all would-be wizards tend to adopt when their competence is questioned, "you may believe that if you like, sir, but I must agree with my esteemed colleague Odo that you have too haughty an attitude to man and God alike."

"Peace!" said Jean Funeste, in a soothing fashion. "It will not help us to become annoyed with one another. Nor will it help us to blame the Lord for what He might or might not have condescended to do by way of enlightenment. My friend is a pious man, but he is surely right to insist that we exhaust rational explanations before coming to the conclusion that there are supernatural forces at work here. Let us think about this logically, and see where rigorous reason might lead us."

"If that is your wish," said Odo, skeptically, "then let us do that—but let us not forget what feeble creatures we are when we are faced with the mysteries of life and death."

"I am as accomplished in calculation as any other astrologer," Furalor said, similarly putting on a show of wounded vanity, "and I am as respectful of evidence and the processes of deduction as any magistrate. If my magic has failed, without more powerful magic being at work, I shall be glad to admit it and pleased to know how. Go on, Master Clerk: I shall follow your logic loyally every step of the way."

"Thank you, gentlemen," said Jean Funeste, evenly. "I do think that there is another way to interpret what has happened here, and with your permission, Monsieur Sevanter, I will explain the logic that leads to the conclusion—although I feel obliged to warn you that you might not like it any better than what these men have said."

"I am a magistrate," replied his friend, stoutly, "and I am very eager to hear all evidence and argument, wherever it may lead."

"Well then," said Jean Funeste, "let us consider the possibility that Furalor's precautions were not so easily evaded. We packed the chests together, you will recall, after taking our last inventory, and then locked them all carefully. Then I left the room in search of the astrologer, did I not, returning some minutes later so that the alarm spells could be set?"

"That is so," said the magistrate. "But I did not leave the room. No one could have removed the objects from the chest before the spell was set."

"But it is possible, so far as I can tell," said the clerk, "that the objects we later found to be missing were not in the chests when the locks alarm was set, having been removed in that interim. Assessing the evidence purely from my own point of view, I cannot testify to the fact that the objects were still in the chests when the alarm spells were set and the cupboard was locked—and the same judgment holds true for the previous night."

"But that is absurd!" exclaimed the magistrate. "I can assure you, Jean, that the objects were *not* removed while you were out of the room. Who could have done that, save for me?"

Jean Funeste spread his arms wide, and said: "There you have it, my friend, in a nutshell: the conclusion to which logic inexorably leads. Who has seen the Phantom inside this house, except yourself? No one. How could the Phantom possibly have entered the room and left it again without my seeing him, since I was very carefully blocking the door and was exceedingly quick to react to your cries for help? Impossible—unless he was a mere figment of your imagination. Who else but you, in fact, could possibly have contrived *any* of the mysterious things that the Phantom is supposed to have done within this house? No one—if the things were, in fact, done rather than merely imagined. Ergo, I feel compelled to ask my companions to give serious consideration to the proposition that you are the one who has done or imagined them!"

Here Jean Funeste was forced to pause, because Monsieur Sevanter appeared likely to suffer a fit of apoplexy. The clerk immediately put a reassuring hand on his friend's shoulder, and said to him in a kindly tone: "Of course, my old friend, I do not say that you have done or imagined these things *knowingly*, but only that you must have done them. You could have conjured up this ghost. You could have taken these various relics of your dead wife from your father's and your children's houses. You could be the Phantom, and it is hard to see that anyone else can have done what the Phantom has done these last two nights. What other explanation is as probable? That you have been bewitched, accursed or otherwise deluded is very probable—indeed, I do not doubt it—but I must, in all conscience, say that, if logic is to be our guide, we cannot seriously doubt that yours are the hands which have actually carried out these actions."

Monsieur Sevanter was of a different opinion. "This is utterly absurd!" he howled, in a rage that would have done credit to a raving lunatic. "It is monstrous! I have been your firmest friend for forty years, Jean Funeste, and now you accuse me of this! I am a victim of robbery and evil haunting, and the only conclusion that my closest friend can reach is that I must have robbed myself and haunted myself! You serpent of ingratitude! Everything you have and everything you are, you owe to my generosity! You were a mere gardener's boy, and I made you a clerk. Do you know how hard I had to work to persuade my parents to let you be my friend? You miserable traitor! Logic be damned! Your contention is the vilest slander I have ever heard, and I only wish that I could find a punishment to fit such a crime, for I would surely exact it on the spot. Leave my house this instant, and take your worthless spell-casters with you. Begone! I shall face this vicious Phantom alone, and I will find out who he is for myself."

It is doubtful that Odo or Furalor would have been over-anxious to agree with the curious hypothesis that Jean Funeste had advanced had it been put to them in calm circumstances, even though it relieved both of them from any hint of responsibility for the misfortunes afflicting the house. Once Monsieur Sevanter had exploded in this remarkable manner, however, compounding his earlier intemperate insults by calling them both worthless, they were by no means so inclined to dispute it. In fact, each of them came independently to the conclusion that Monsieur Sevanter was as excessive in his ingratitude as he was in his impoliteness, and that Jean Funeste's charges, however unlikely they might have seemed at first, must have struck a spot made sore by conscience.

Jean Funeste, on the other hand, seemed to repent his reckless words completely, and hastened to offer a thousand apologies for having hurt his friend's feelings. Indeed, he begged to be allowed to remaining the house—in order, as he put it, to help Monsieur Sevanter defend himself against himself. This manner of representing the situation only served to rouse Monsieur Sevanter's anger to a higher pitch, and he would not be content until his former friend was banished from his house. Jean Funeste had to leave, in order to avoid being thrown out bodily. Furalor and Odo went with him, both feeling somewhat aggrieved by the way that their sincere attempts to help had not been better appreciated.

In spite of the rough way he had been treated, Jean Funeste was careful to make a copy of his report on the previous night's occurrences, and he took Odo and Furalor with him to present it to the mayor and Paul Mansard. He did not include an account of his final conversation with the magistrate in his written report, but he did explain his thesis to the merchant and the mayor. Odo and Furalor confirmed that this verbal account was accurate, and added their own endorsements to Jean Funeste's logical conclusion.

"I fear," said Furalor, sorrowfully, "that our beloved magistrate has gone mad. He is seeing things that are not there—indeed, he is shooting at things that are not there. He stealing from his own treasure-chests, and blaming the thefts of a product of his imagination. Perhaps there is black magic at work, but I doubt it. Monsieur

Sevanter may need to be committed to the lunatic asylum in Is, if he is not to be held accountable in law for what he has done."

"Furalor is right," said Odo, decisively. "Magic is probably not involved; the ghost is a mere hallucination of Monsieur Sevanter's enfevered brain; the clandestine removal of the objects from the chests is proof of that. There is no demonic possession here, and no witchcraft—but there is madness; of that I have no doubt. The lunatic asylum might be the answer, if the punishment decreed by law is to be avoided."

"These worthy gentlemen are undoubtedly justified in their conclusion," Jean Funeste put in, "but I feel, gentlemen, that they are being a little harsh. That my old friend has been driven to the end of his tether, and that his mind has given way to some degree, are undeniable. There has always been madness in his family, as you know, and his robust appearance should not cause us to forget that he is heir to a long tradition of inbreeding and degeneracy—but when we take that into account, we must acknowledge that Monsieur Sevanter has actually held up far better than could have been expected under the burden of his long service to the ideals of justice. I have been alongside him as he worked throughout these last twenty-five years, and I can testify to the pressure put on the imagination by the ceaselessly exposure to crime and criminals. All the horrors that lurk beneath the surface of Teirbrun's society eventually become manifest in its court-room, in which Monsieur Sevanter has heroically borne the burden of magistracy, on his own, for an entire generation. It is not unnatural that he should become a little unbalanced, after all that time—but what we are dealing with is a matter of slight imbalance, curable by rest. He does not need to be committed to an asylum, and I, Jean Funeste, will not hear of any such horrid eventuality. What he needs is to go home, to his father's house, for three months. During that time, Monsieur Mayor, you must apply to the Royal Court of Is to be replaced on the circuit of its Court of Assizes—purely as a temporary measure, of course."

"That's all very well," the ever-pragmatic Paul Mansard put in, "but where's the loot?"

"I beg your pardon, sir?" said Jean Funeste.

"Where are all the things that the Phantom has stolen? Can they be recovered? Can restitution be made?"

"Ah!" said Jean Funeste. "Well, sir, I can testify that the Phantom's spoils are not hidden in Monsieur Sevanter's house—I know every last nook and cranny of it. Logic suggests that they must be hidden somewhere in his father's house, or its grounds. If the mayor can spare a few constables, perhaps a discreet search might be mounted. I should have thought of it myself—it would provide the final proof of the chain of reasoning."

"I'll do it," the mayor was quick to say. "Better than that—I'll supervise the search personally. Nothing would give me greater pleasure than to restore their property to the citizens of my town."

"I can believe that," Paul Mansard observed.

"But in the meantime, gentlemen," Jean Funeste, "I must ask you to promise not to make any further move against Monsieur Sevanter. We must protect him as carefully from himself as we would protect him from any malicious enemy, and must nurse him through this crisis in his affairs. Tonight, he expects to confront the Phantom for the last time; if he comes through that crisis alive and well, I believe we shall be able to restore him to health without any need to think in terms of the lunatic asylum."

"You have ever been a good and steadfast friend to my son-in-law, Master Funeste" said Paul Mansard. "I am sure that the mayor will take no further action without consulting you, no matter how lowly your supposed status might be."

"Certainly not," the mayor hastened to say. "The Town Council will be very glad to have your advice, Master Clerk."

VII.

By nightfall, the story of the quarrel between Alphonse Sevanter and Jean Funeste was all around the town, as was the starling revelation that the notorious Phantom was none other than Monsieur Sevanter himself, who had gone mad. Many of the poorer folk—especially those who had come under suspicion by virtue of their own past misdemeanors or those of their relatives—immediately began to assert that he had been mad for years, and that his peculiar sentencing policies had been clear evidence of the slow but steady corruption of his brain. Some, however, asserted that he was not mad at all, but had simply turned to a life of crime by virtue of his excessive arrogance and manifest impiety. Even a few people of quality, who had never imagined such a possibility, ventured to say that they had always suspected something, and had long feared that some such crisis might materialize eventually.

Shortly after nightfall, another rumor began to make the rounds, to the effect that the mayor himself had supervised a search by town constables of the grounds of the so-called Manse d'Ys, and that they had found a substantial cache of stolen valuables hidden in the carefully-shaped ornamental bushes of the so-called Duc's garden. Although no detailed inventory had yet been made, it seemed likely that the greater part of the gems and silver-plate stolen by the Phantom would soon be returned to his victims, although the cash had all been spent and the comestibles consumed. The instruments of domestic discipline and most of the weapons also seemed to be missing.

This new rumor probably set a new speed record in traveling through the space within the town's walls, save for one tiny black spot; no one brought it to the attention of Monsieur Sevanter. Jean Funeste's request that the Great Judge be let alone, in order that no further pressure should be added to his climactic confrontation with his inner demons, was universally honored.

Jean Funeste and Paul Mansard went to the magistrate's house together in order to speak to all the watchmen and servants within its grounds, although Odo and Furalor had declined a request to accompany them. Jean Funeste impressed upon all the servants the absolute necessity of leaving Monsieur Sevanter to himself, save for the customary duties that they were obliged to carry out, and he insisted that these duties should be carried out with the utmost efficiency and quietness.

"Your master will not hang for the crimes that he has unwittingly committed," the clerk assured Monsieur Sevanter's staff, "nor will he be committed to the asylum in Is. Your positions are quite safe, provided that you exercise the utmost discretion until this tragic matter can be settled—which it will be, I hope and expect, tomorrow."

"If you can take care of the situation here, Master Funeste," Paul Mansard added, "I will take all the necessary measures to return the man items of stolen property to Monsieur Sevanter's victims, and add up the sums in cash of which he will need to make restitution—covering food and wine too, of course."

"You have always been a good friend to Monsieur Sevanter, sir," said Jean Funeste, "and I am extremely glad to have your assistance in this tortuous matter."

Thanks to the tireless efforts of Jean Funeste, Monsieur Sevanter went to bed that night as tranquil as any man in his situation could possibly be. He knew that he was a less admirable man, in the estimation of his poorer neighbors, than he had been before, but he did not know the extent to which his reputation had been tarnished in the eyes of his own class. In his own mind, he was absolutely certain that he was not guilty of the perverse charges that Funeste had so unexpectedly leveled against him, and he was very enthusiastic to prove it in whatever manner he could. He was looking forward with feverish anticipation to the Phantom's promised return, and was determined to capture him this time, alive or dead.

Better to capture him alive, the magistrate told himself, *in order that he can tell us what magic he used to work his seeming miracles—but better to have him dead than not to have him at all.*

He distributed his servants about the house as before, placed the four watchmen that still remained to him about the grounds, and carefully checked the locks on all his doors—including his bedroom door, which would now require a better guard than Jean Funeste's hammock—and all his windows. He gathered all the keys together under his pillow, along with the pistol. He did not waste any effort on such frippery as "magical alarms".

Before he went to bed, though, the magistrate carefully searched through one of the treasure-chests and removed from it a small oval portrait of his dead wife, which had been painted before their marriage, and presented to him as a token of her respect. She had ever been a respectful woman, who had never taken advantage of their intimacy to excuse any lapse of politeness. He could not be entirely certain that the portrait was the article most likely to be sought by the Phantom in his final raid, but it seemed altogether likely. He locked the chest and the cupboard again, and then placed the portrait and the keys beneath his pillow. He lit five wax candles, as he had on the previous night.

Having carefully inspected the bullet-hole in the paneling of his bedroom wall, Monsieur Sevanter was by now convinced that he had missed his shot on the previous night because he had failed to hold the pistol's barrel straight when he was startled by the smoke and the recoil, but that he could only have missed hitting the Phantom by a mere whisker. He was determined that his hand should be steady enough this time, if he had the opportunity to fire another shot.

The process of taking these precautions, with minute care, calmed the magistrate's anxiety somewhat, but they could not entirely quiet his residual wrath at the suggestion that his persecution was all in his mind. He did, however, conclude that he might have over-reacted when Jean Funeste had made the suggestion, given that the poor fellow had indeed, only been tracing a chain of reasoning, and had assured his friend that he did not believe for a moment that the Great Judge had deceived anyone intentionally. Despite forming a resolution to forgive his old friend, though, he felt as he went to bed as if an iron band had been drawn around his waist, squeezing his belly.

His head seemed calm enough when he first laid it on the pillow, but it did not stay calm for long. Before an hour had elapsed it had turned into a seething cauldron of thoughts and images, with wild ideas bursting randomly like punctured soap-bubbles within his consciousness. He did not need to fall asleep to fall prey to a menacing delirium.

Two images from his previous nightmares kept coming back to him while he waited: the image of the graveyard in which the dead were rising from their tombs, bent on keeping their appointment with the man who had sentenced them to death; and the image of his long-dead wife, as contained in the portrait beneath his pillow.

Because these images kept rising into his mind, in spite the fact that he was still awake, he forced himself to search for something more solid to look at, fixing his eyes in turn upon the locked door, the windows, and the place in the opposite wall where the bullet had struck. Finally, though, he took the portrait from his pillow, and occupied himself in staring at the face of the young girl whose wise and careful father had done him the honor of accepting his most generous offer for her hand.

Remarkably, the sight of the picture calmed him more than anything else he had looked at. As he stared into the painted eyes, he became convinced that, if this really was the face of the fiend that haunted him, then the ghost had certainly not risen of its own volition, but had been torn from its rest by the foulest necromancy.

But that, he thought, *can hardly be possible. So-called magic is all delusion, all trickery. I am an educated man and a student of the law. Jean Funeste was correct in one thing, although he was drawn to a false conclusion by some mistaken premise: the key to this affair is reason, not superstition, and logic will solve it, if only it is correctly and wisely applied.*

Having reached this conclusion, Monsieur Sevanter found himself thinking more lucidly again, like a Great Judge and as a man of unusual cleverness and wit. He realized then how clouded his mind had been before—for days rather than hours—by wrath and irritation.

And then, quite suddenly, he saw everything that had happened in a clearer light, and understood, beyond a shadow of a doubt, who the Phantom must be.

Monsieur Sevanter looked up then, and saw that the Phantom was already with him, standing at the foot of the bed, looking at him, exactly as he had on the previous night and the night before that, through the holes of his mask. In the glow of the five candles, the Phantom seemed a good deal clearer this time than he had before, but the loose-hanging cloak still hid his body, while the black silk mask and the hood concealed his face and hair. All of that, Monsieur Sevanter decided, grimly, would only serve to make him a more obvious target

Monsieur Sevanter took out the pistol, as he had on the previous night, and pointed it at the mask, but did not hasten to fire. "My hand is much steadier tonight, Jean Funeste," he said. "I promise that you I will not miss again, now that I know who and what you are."

Jean Funeste released a slight sigh, and then reached up without delay to remove the mask from his face and the hood from his head, as if he were tired of the masquerade. He dropped the mask on the floor, but tucked the hood carefully away inside the clothes he was wearing under the cloak. Monsieur Sevanter had the distinct impression that it was not the same cloak that the Phantom had worn on the previous two occasions—which would make sense, if the other one had merely been a blue night-shirt turned inside out, facilitating the clerk's rapid transformation from apparent haunter to apparent ally.

In the meantime, Jean Funeste looked at the magistrate with eyes as hard as flints, and said: "I knew that you would work it out once I had shown you the way—but I knew that you would have to calm down first, giving me time to complete my work. You should not try to kill me, for I have not tried to kill you. I deserve a more ingeniously fitting punishment, just as you have"

Alphonse Sevanter licked his lips, and stared into the naked face of the man who was most definitely no longer his friend, and must have been his enemy for far longer than he cared to think.

"I admit that you have been very ingenious in planning this assassination of my character, Jean" he whispered, "but I deny that I have committed any crime that deserves such a horrid and convoluted punishment—or, indeed, any crime at all. No, I should not try to kill you, and I will not, provided that you behave yourself. You are the villain in this matter, and everyone in Teirbrun will know it by nightfall tomorrow. I shall have you in my court before the week is out—and all your victims will be there to see what ingenious punishment I might contrive."

"Perhaps," said Jean Funeste. "If it will reassure you, I promise that I shall not try to run away this time. When your servants burst through that door to seize the Phantom, I shall be here, standing meekly by the bed. In the meantime, I shall be glad to enlighten you as to the crimes you have committed, and the revenge that they demanded. You no longer need to be enlightened, I suppose, as to the means by which I stole your possessions."

"Logic did that," the magistrate replied, calmly. "The same logic that you used to demonstrate that, from your point of view, only I could have done it, served to demonstrate that, from mine, only you could have done it. When you left the room after taking the inventory, you took the items with you, heaving secreted them about your person by sleight of hand. I should have realized that immediately—or, indeed, two days ago—but I thought that you were above suspicion. Whatever secret hatreds you have nursed, you must allow that I have always trusted you implicitly. I have always treated you with the utmost condescension, in spite of the difference in our stations, and never suspected you capable of the horrid envy that you must have harbored all along. I am a generous and kindly man, Jean—worthier by far than you have turned out to be."

"I agree that you have always treated me with the utmost condescension," said Funeste, "and I am well aware of the extent to which you overestimate your worth as a man, while remaining blithely unaware of your own failings."

Monsieur Sevanter's finger tightened a little on the trigger of his weapon, but he did not press it. He was no longer frightened, now that he knew who it was that he had to face, but he was genuinely disappointed.

"I truly thought you were my friend, Jean," he said, sadly. "Why were you not my friend, when I was always such a good friend to you?"

"You hold the answer in your hand," replied Jean Funeste.

Monsieur Sevanter looked down at the pistol—but then he realized that the clerk must mean the other hand, which was still gripping the portrait of his dead wife.

"I could have forgiven you the rest," the clerk said. "I could have forgiven you for winning every other contest in which we took part as boys or men, by virtue of the unearned start in life that your station gave you, even though I was always the stronger and the cleverer of us. I could have forgiven you for becoming a magistrate while I remained a clerk, even though my understanding of the law was superior to yours. I could even have forgiven you for becoming famous for all those cunning sentences you passed, which earned you the title of the Great Judge, although more than three in every four were ideas that I put into your head. I was always the man who fit punishments neatly to crimes—and I still am. I am merely taking my career to its logical conclusion."

Sevanter looked down at the portrait that he held in his hand. "I remember that you liked her," he said, quietly.

"Liked her!" said Funeste, stifling a cry of pain and showing for the first time the torment that he must have kept hidden for many long years. "I *loved* her, with all my heart—and she loved me! But you were a magistrate and I was your clerk. There was little gold in your family coffers, but you were a man of importance, especially in town like Teirbrun. There was not a shred of silver in my purse, and I could never be anything more in Teirbrun than your faithful shadow. She loved me, but she would not marry for love. Her father would never have permitted it, of course, but that question never arose. Had it only been a matter of his prohibition, I could have reconciled myself to the inevitability—but it was not. She would not even entertain the thought. She would rather have a man without a heart, whose fine clothes and full pockets made up for the emptiness that was inside him. If *you* had loved her as I loved her, I would have thought you blameless, and would gladly have forgiven her, but you did not. You never saw beyond the matter of mere business that you completed with her father. I could not forgive you what you are, and what you made of her."

"But men of my sort cannot marry for love!" said the Great Judge, with the air of one stating the obvious. "Love is a last resort when it comes to reasons for marriage. It is reason that sets human beings above the beasts, and we must live by that reason and not as slaves to silly passion. The poor sometimes marry for love, because they cannot marry for gain, but they would not do it if they had the choice."

"Your daughter married for love," Jean Funeste pointed out.

"And suffered the consequences," Monsieur Sevanter retorted. "My father was displeased with me, as you know, for marrying Blanche—he considered her station too far beneath me—but you argued very cogently on my behalf, as I recall, regarding the economic wisdom of the alliance."

"I did," Jean Funeste agreed. "And every word was true, as regards the *economic* wisdom of the alliance. Had your father once raised the objection, though, that you did not love her, or that she did not love you, I would have confessed myself beaten and admitted that he was correct in his opposition. He did not. His arguments were as blind to the reality of human emotion and human worth as yours."

"You're a fool, Jean," said the magistrate, sadly. "I always suspected you of reading poetry when we should have been studying our law books."

"I had time to do that," Jean Funeste told him, "because I was more intelligent than you, and more efficient in my studies."

"Hardly more *efficient*," Monsieur Sevanter retorted, "since you wasted the time you gained with such trash. You'd have done better to study religious tracts, or mathematics—or astrology, since you obviously could not tolerate too much truth."

"I am more tolerant of the truth than you imagine," Jean Funeste replied, "although I have certainly taken care in spinning a complex web of deception these last few weeks. I was afraid, at first, that you might correlate the Phantom's crimes with my absence from your presence, but you never even noticed my absences, any more than you ever really noticed my presence. I was never anything more than an item of the furniture of your life, which you never really noticed—just as *she* was."

Monsieur Sevanter looked at the portrait again. "Why did you steal her gifts to my children?" he asked.

"Because they should have been gifts to *my* children. It should have been *my* children that she bore, and not yours. You have no right to these things I have taken—you have no right to your own family, though I know you would not care a jot if they were taken away, and so I have not sought to hurt them, or your father either. I loved her. All her love-tokens are rightly mine, and all the things that she loved herself."

"Oh Jean," said the magistrate, with a sigh, "you are a great fool. I truly was your friend, and you ought to have tried harder to be mine. Instead, you have become a famous robber and a faithless betrayer. How shall we ever find a punishment to fit such crimes?"

"We are not here to pass judgment on me," said Jean Funeste. "I have been occupied in passing sentence on *you*. In the eyes of the people of Teirbrun you, not I, are the famous robber. My denunciation was carried to every covert and corner of the town, and because it came from your trusted friend, it was believed! Most of the imperishable valuables that I stolen from the houses of my victims have already been unearthed in your father's garden—which is, to be strictly accurate, *my* father's garden, although no one in Teirbrun will think about that. Your confession, dictated to me in your final hour of life, and signed by your own hand, will also be offered in evidence—I have it in my pocket now, with your name already forged. All of this will be believed, even if you deny it until you are blue in the face, for the mayor and the Town Council—following the sage advice of Furalor and Odo—are already intent on committing you to the lunatic asylum in Is. You are perfectly free to tell the truth, but no one will ever believe you, because my lies have already taken root, and are invulnerable."

"They would not be invulnerable if you were dead," said Monsieur Sevanter. "You are wearing the Phantom's costume, and doubtless carrying the Phantom's dagger. By the time that you were found, with a bullet in your chest, the only signed confession in your pocket would be your own. I can write, you know, even though I have spent a lifetime allowing you to do it for me."

"Alas," said Jean Funeste, in a sympathetic tone, "I believe that you are wrong. I have done my work better than you can imagine. Even if I were found dead, wearing the Phantom's cloak, with a forged confession in its inner pocket, the mayor and Paul Mansard would still be inclined to suspect you, and would surely send you to the asylum in order to be on the safe side. Your only hope of avoiding that fate is to throw yourself on my mercy—for I have promised both of them that I can restore you to your old self, if I am given a free hand. The punishment must fit the crime, you see—I hope that you might condescend to accept my kindness as well as my revenge. I have foreseen every possible eventuality, you see."

"Not quite," said Monsieur Sevanter. "I have not the slightest intention of obliging you by endorsing your lie. Even if shooting you dead did not give me an opportunity to save myself and my reputation—as it surely will—I would certainly derive a good deal of satisfaction from it." And so saying, he fired his weapon, utterly determined this time that the smoke and the recoil would not affect his aim.

The pistol blew up in his hand. The force of the explosion sent fragments of twisted metal into his eyes, cheeks and forehead. More than one tiny sliver penetrated to a deeper level, killing him on the instant.

Jean Funeste had raised his arms to shield himself from the explosion, but he quickly lowered them again.

"Every possible eventuality," he repeated, already beginning to shed the outermost layer of his clothing with swift efficiency. "You should have remembered that it was I who gave you the pistol, adjusted its firing mechanism, and loaded it. You have no idea how many guns I had to steal before I found two identical pieces of which I could be perfectly certain—and to find them in a pork-butcher's, of all places! But I have no time to waste, for the servants will be hammering on the door very shortly." He had another set of clothes on beneath the phantom's cloak, which he moved under the bed with the toe of his shoe. He fell silent as soon as the hammering on the door began, thinking it best not to speak his thoughts aloud from then on.

The clerk unlocked the door, and threw up his hands in feigned despair. "Alas," he cried, in a broken voice "the poor man was so deluded and deranged that he thought his phantom had come back to haunt him again. But look! It is only a portrait of his dear late wife." So saying, he picked up the little picture, bloodstained now, which had fallen on the floor.

When the servants had all looked at it, and nodded their heads in wise appreciation of its significance, in the context of an incurable madness, Jean Funeste put it in his own pocket, and took it away with him.

VIII.

Monsieur Sevanter's clerk was entirely correct in his estimation that the people of Teirbrun would believe everything he told them, and he now had very abundant apparent proofs with which to dispel any residual doubt that any one of them might have harbored He pretended to be so stricken by grief that he never served again as a clerk to the court of Teirbrun, but retired to live in solitude in the depths of the forest of Leonais, alone with his memories and his secrets.

Alphonse Sevanter, who was famous while he lived as the Great Judge, became more famous still after his death, albeit rather briefly, as the Phantom Who Haunted Himself. It was said of him by many of his former acquaintances that he had reserved the most fiendish of all his ingenious punishments for himself.

Whether Jean Funeste was damned to Hell for the sins he had committed in devising, as he saw it, a penalty uniquely fitted to his enemy's trespasses, no one can possibly know. All that is certain is that he died only a few years after, but that, immediately before he died, he made a full confession of the whole affair—not to any priestly confessor but to a wandering story-teller like myself, whom he first forced to swear that the tale should never, under any circumstances, be told within the walls of Teirbrun.

The inevitable result of that injunction, of course, was that everyone within those walls had heard the whole of it within a fortnight—and the most wretched members of the poorest classes were, for once, united with the most pretentious members of the highest in thinking it the finest tale to which their ancient town had ever given birth.

CUSTER'S LAST STAND

Custer rolled out of bed feeling like one of Dada's furry tea-cups. He blinked, and directed a hostile glare at the thin stream of sunlight that crept through the crack between the curtains.

Perhaps they've gone, he thought, breaking last night's firm resolution within seconds of opening his eyes. He had resolved that he wouldn't even *think* about them until he was dressed and suitably fortified by a Weetabix with marmalade and a strong cup of coffee. As things turned out, though, he staggered into the bathroom thinking about them every step of the way.

Why me? he appealed to the mirror. *What have I done to deserve this kind of treatment.*

He left the curtains closed while he ate breakfast. It was getting to the point that he was afraid to touch a curtain. The ones in the bedroom stayed closed permanently. He made the coffee last, not too proud to seize any legitimate excuse to delay going to the window and confronting the morning. The coffee helped build up his courage, largely because of the healthy slug of Irish whiskey he used instead of milk. It was early in the day, by his standards: hardly half past eleven.

When the last dregs of the coffee were gone, the comfortable uncertainty had to end. He had to find out. He strode to the window and hurled back the curtains with a single convulsive jerk. A mighty flourish, as he might himself have described it.

They were still there.

There were eight this morning, all but one armed with placards. They were not marching—not even bothering to obstruct the pavement. There was no point. Since the demonstration had begun nobody had attempted to use that particular stretch of pavement. Everyone crossed the road to avoid them. Four of them were sitting on the garden wall with their backs to Custer. One leaned against the gatepost, staring moodily at the road. Two were propped up by his car, which was parked in the drive with its hind end projecting beyond the gateposts. The eighth one—the ringleader—was walking slowly up and down between the invisible boundary lines that could have been constructed by imaginatively extending the twin garden hedges.

When Custer drew back the curtains and stood looking at them, with mixed fear and fury, they turned round one by one to stare at him. They twirled the handles of the placards so that each legend was facing him. As he read them—one or two for the first time, because some had been renewed overnight—all the anger and frustration bubbled up inside him. He licked his lips.

Little Dorothy Gretton, who had been savagely raped in *Subscription to Sin*, carried a placard that read CLEAN UP CUSTER—mild and trite, like the character herself. She was looking pale and harassed, and Custer remembered that, after carefully engineering and orchestrating her rape, he had described a "shadow in her eyes that haunted her face for the rest of her days." The thought of the word "haunted" made him wince.

Strangely enough, the man sitting next to little Dorothy on the wall was Valentine Wrinch, who had perpetrated the evil deed. He still had some nasty scars on his face, which had been inflicted when, in the course of the climactic chase scene, he had run full tilt into a barbed wire fence. Custer seemed to remember that he had deftly plucked out one of Wrinch's eyes with that fence, but the stare that transfixed him now was definitely two-eyed. The cursed ghosts couldn't even be *consistent*. Wrinch's placard read: CUSTER'S CRUELTY INTOLERABLE.

Hector Nettleship, who had turned out after 147 suspense-filled pages to be *The Groping Ghoul* (and had spent the next twenty pages relating in grotesque detail to Fay Hartshorn the experiences in nursery school that were responsible for his taking the wrong path in life) carried the message: CUSTER'S BOOKS ARE FILTH.

Rita Costello from the classic *Kiss of Corruption*—which was still his all-time best-seller—had WE DEMAND FAIR PLAY. Moira Thilly, the lovesick moron who had been one of his authentic masterpieces of negative characterization in *Fury in the Fog*, had a suitably simple-minded scrawl, which simply said: CUSTER UNFAIR TO CHARACTERS.

Lucia Cartwright, arguably the prettiest and most likeable character he had ever created—for his adolescent, rather over-sentimental drama *Harlot's Hearse*—was the showpiece of the group. *Harlot's Hearse* had been his first book and had been a dismal failure until later books, achieving best-seller status, had led to its reprinting. Lucia had suffered with a kind of dignity that Custer would not have permitted in his more mature work. She had no stab-wounds, acid-burns or even dark shadows in her eyes to mar her glossy perfection. Her banner said IMAGINARY PEOPLE HAVE FEELINGS TOO.

The last placard, carried by Josh Black—the strong-arm man who had proved so fearsomely successful in *Beauty and the Brute*—read: WE DEMAND A REWRITE.

The man who carried no message for Custer and the world was the only one who wore a smile as he looked his creator in the eye. He had no right to do that, because, in all the 252 pages of *Accursed Humanity!*—Custer's attempt to write a commentary on the human condition that would stand alongside the greatest literary works of all time—Jonathan Shaw had never smiled once.

Custer gave Shaw the filthiest look imaginable—one that would have defied even *his* powers of description—and turned on his heel.

I'll get you for this, Shaw, he subvocalised. *Just wait until I write the bloody sequel!*

* * * * * *

The ghosts were fairly real—which is to say, they were more real than they would have been if Custer alone could see them, but less real than they would have been if people could touch them as well. They were, in technical language, visible but not tangible. This had become comically apparent when a policeman, in response to

Custer's complaint that there was a gang of cut-throats loitering with intent outside his house, had tried to move them on. The long arm of the law had gone straight through the demonstrators. Even the placards were only visual images.

Unfortunately for Custer, the ghosts could be heard as well as seen. They held press conferences. Within a matter of hours after the picketing had first started the whole world was informed of his predicament. The papers had at first refused to print anything substantial, because it sounded so ridiculous, but after Jonathan Shaw appeared on *Nationwide*, and a famous skeptic was called upon to pass his hands through Shaw's body in front of several million viewers, they relented in no uncertain terms. Gigantic headlines had announced the news: BEST-SELLER'S CHARACTERS OUT ON STRIKE. A group of building workers occupying a site in Cricklewood in protest against the fact that several of them had accidentally been issued Wellingtons with two left feet had gone back to work. They felt that they couldn't realistically compete for the sympathy of the public—and they were right.

For a week after the strike began, sightseers flocked to watch the various demonstrations. They gathered outside Custer's house for the big show, but soon discovered that there were pickets outside the offices of his publisher and his agent and the home of the only man who had ever given him a good review. There were also pickets outside every branch of W. H. Smith's up and down the country, and by the busiest railway stations as well. Being intangible, they couldn't actually stop people buying Custer's books, but they could certainly make such transactions damnably embarrassing. The first major victory won by the pickets was that of persuading various bookshop managers to take Custer's manifold works off display, so that they became available only on request.

Custer had thought, optimistically, that the blaze of publicity would result in unprecedented sales, and for a while it did, but as the strike dragged on, popular interest in the ghosts overtook interest in the books from whose pages they had come. Endless sympathetic interviews with the characters, and a multitude of harrowing pictures showing how Custer had cruelly mutilated them in the course of the violent climaxes for which he was so celebrated, gradually turned public opinion against Custer. By the time the strike was a month old some of his most devoted fans would not have been seen dead with one of his books in their hands.

One old lady in Heckmondwyke, a small town in Yorkshire, publicly burned her extensive collection of first editions, including an autographed copy of *Blood and Guts*. Second-hand dealers suddenly found Custer to be a drug on the market, and Oxfam shops refused to accept copies as gifts. The worst aspect of the tragedy was, however, purely personal. Since the strike began, Custer had found himself unable to write a single line of the florid prose that had made him famous. The characters didn't even wait until he began putting them on paper. They just got right up out of his head and walked out to join the strikers, at which point the pickets on duty outside the house would cheer madly.

Jonathan Shaw and the others insisted publicly, of course, that they were *not* preventing Custer from writing, but were simply not going to stand for the kind of writing in which he habitually indulged. They wanted him to write *nice* stories, with strong characters and upbeat endings, in which not a single character was, as Shaw put it, "vilely abused". But where, Custer wanted to scream at them—and occasionally had—was the drama in that? Where was the suspense? Where was the nerve-jangling tension that kept his readers on the edges of their seats, with their hearts pounding?

Such arguments cut no ice with Shaw, or any of his fellow strikers. They wanted an end to Custer's "authorial sadism", and they were determined to get it.

The strike was about eleven weeks old now, and most of the sightseers had long since become bored. The only people lurking on the far side of the road now, watching the interminable vigil, were sixteen Japanese tourists on a package tour and an old lady who had brought her favorite granddaughter.

"One of those men has a pair of scissors sticking out of his back," said the grandchild, in shrill but contemplative tones. She obviously knew better than to mention the blood that was dripping from Moira Thilly's skirt, in case Granny might think that sight unsuitable for her innocent eyes.

"It's only a pretend pair of scissors," the old lady assured the little girl. "That's Hector Nettleship."

"How do you know?" asked the little girl.

Granny, who knew it because she had read *The Groping Ghoul* six times, declined to answer that.

"If they're only pretend scissors," said the grandchild, "why does he keep *groaning* all the time?"

"He has a *tortured soul*," said Granny, remembering Custer's phrase exactly. "But only a *pretend* tortured soul," she added, hastily.

* * * * * * *

Custer was a tough man. At least, he was a tough-minded man. He approved of corporal punishment for football hooligans and thought that the government ought to outsource the prison service to whichever Third World nation cared to put in the lowest tender. On the one occasion when he had been threatened with personal violence by a teenage mugger, however, he had fainted. He did have courage of a kind, though. He was determined not to give in to the demands of his rebel characters. He *believed* in his writing. It was a sacred vocation.

He had already contracted to write his next book, with the provisional title *Evil Ecstasy*, but he had been able to make no headway with it at all. Nowadays, he didn't even bother starting the day by typing the title all over again. Nevertheless, he sat down at the Adler MX electric typewriter that he persisted in using, in spite of the ready availability of word-processors, because it somehow reflected the kind of no-nonsense down-to-earth writer that he was. He threaded in the paper (two carbons), and paused for thought.

While he paused, he poured himself a drink.

For a few seconds, his mind was a blank, but he coaxed it into action by throwing back the whiskey at a single gulp.

His fingers flew as, one-third of the way down the page and imperfectly centered, he typed: *The Disintegration of Jonathan Shaw*. Underneath it—double-spaced, of course—he added: *by Marcus Custer*.

Disintegration was good, he thought. Death was too good for the bastard, and so was dismembering. Besides which, *nobody* used words like "dismembering" in a title. He had, at various times past, contemplated burning Shaw alive or having him eaten by piranhas, but the direct method seemed best. Things had to be ironed out while the strike was hot.

He had a strong sense of *déjà-vu* as he spaced in for the first paragraph and brought up his hands like a conductor about to launch into Beethoven's Fifth or Strauss's *Also Sprach Zarathustra*.

He tried to think. No messing about. Never mind the build-up, just get on with the plot. Disintegrate the bastard on the first page....in the first line, even.

But somehow, he just couldn't construct such a sentence in his imagination. The reason was simple. Jonathan Shaw, character, was no longer *in* Custer's imagination. He was outside, leading the revolution.

Custer had the worst writer's block in literary history.

The phone on the desk began to ring. Custer looked at it as if it were a tarantula crawling out of a packet of cheese and onion crisps.

There was just a slight possibility that it was a genuine call, and he absolutely refused to give up hope. He lifted the receiver and held it slightly away from him, trying to find out who it was before putting it to his ear.

"Custer," hissed a masculine voice, "you're a no-good shit. You stink."

Custer lost his temper. "You can't do this to me!" he yelled, unrealistically. His nerveless fingers refused to slam down the phone. Even more horrible than the fact that he kept getting these calls was the fact that he didn't know who was making them. It might be Mervyn Vetch out of *Dial Depravity* or Nigel Sellars of *Torture by Telephone*. In a not-uncharacteristic burst of unconscious self-plagiarism Custer had described the voices of both phone freaks in exactly the same terms. It was not humanly possible to tell them apart.

"For years you've been getting away with it," hissed Vetch/Sellars, "but not any more. We've got you where we want you. No more murder. No more sadism. No more exploitation of the innocent figments of your imagination. You're washed up, Custer. You've plotted your last atrocity, sublimated your last perverted urge. Your cesspit mind is as naked as Daisy Gates on page 35 of *Dial Depravity*. All your corruption is on show. Everyone can see you now for what you really are."

"You...," said Custer, stuttering slightly while he wondered whether the reference to *Dial Depravity* meant that the caller was Vetch or whether it was a red herring to torment and delude him. "You *disgusting* creature! How dare you plague me like this! You're *sick*. You're *evil*."

"And whose fault is that?" crowed the ambiguous voice.

"Look, Vetch," said Custer, in more controlled tones. "Or Sellars, or whoever. If it wasn't for me you wouldn't exist at all. I put you in a million homes, made you famous. Do you know how many *real* obscene phone callers were reported to be using *your* dialogue...dialogue that *I* wrote for you? Not ten, not twenty, but *forty-seven*. Or thirty-five, depending on whether you're Vetch or Sellars. Anyhow, a lot. I put you on the map. I got you the attention that all phone freaks crave for."

"Cut the psychological crap, Custer," snarled the caller. "You gave me a mind that would make any self-respecting shrink vomit on his Rorschach blots. I'm the laughing stock of every mental hospital north of the Watford Gap. *Nobody* has a mind like mine except all the other sex-starved, brain-washed, ego-castrated, blood-obsessed characters who populate your vicious little best-sellers. And we don't like it, you hear? We won't put up with it any longer."

"It's not true!" retorted Custer. "What about Maurice Bosanquet in *Parasites of Passion*? I have six letters from genuine certified schizophrenics telling me that they'd never *begun* to understand themselves before they read that book. I have *insight*, damn you. I understand the true nature of the human mind. What do shrinks know? Neurotics, the lot of them. Writers were exploring the hidden recesses of the human psyche while Freud was still sitting on his potty and refusing to shit. I know what makes people tick. My books are authentic comments on the social reality of today."

"Crap," replied Vetch/Sellars. "You got a dirty mind, and that's all."

"I've got *readers*," said Custer. "I've got *fans*. There are people who depend on me, because the experience of reading my books is the only thrill that ever invades their stupid, boring lives. There are people who think that I'm the greatest thing that ever happened to English literature."

"Poor sods," said the caller, and hung up.

Custer put the phone back on the hook. He didn't dare leave it off. It was his last potential contact with the real world. Nobody had crossed the picket line in a fortnight—not even the delivery boy from the wine merchant's. He was desperately afraid that next time he took the car down to the supermarket they would refuse to let him in. The manager had already complained that the inevitable retinue of gruesome ghosts made his sales staff nervous.

He poured himself another drink: a large one.

* * * * * * *

In Cambridge, a man carrying a copy of *Vile Victims* on Market Hill was seized by a group of militant students, who forced him to eat the title page. It was only the uniform paperback edition, but it proved rather indigestible and the man was forced to take an Alka-Seltzer as soon as he got home.

In Hampstead a group of frightened writers held an emergency meeting of the *ad hoc* committee that had been set up by the Society of Authors to investigate the situation. Three independent witnesses reported having seen Tarzan on Oxford Street during the Saturday morning shopping crowd. Luella Townsend claimed to be a nervous wreck on account of seeing girls who might be any one of her multitudinous heroines every time she walked down the street. A rival acidly suggested that Luella's characters had always lacked individuality. A suggestion from an aged writer of detective stories that the group should call upon Sherlock Holmes to figure out the situation was dismissed by the committee. The only science fiction writer present sat alone in a corner muttering fervently to himself: "You think *you've* got problems. Oh Jesus, oh Jesus!"

A very moral saleslady in the Coventry Cathedral Bookshop refused primly to sell a customer in a shabby raincoat a copy of *De-*

generate Delight. "Please," begged the customer, with tears in his eyes. "The public shouldn't be made to suffer because of a petty industrial dispute. What about essential supplies to hospitals? My aunt's in an iron lung and I know she'll just *die* if I can't get her a Marcus Custer for her birthday. She'd just lose all interest in living. It's not as if I wanted it for myself. She's always claimed that Marcus Custer kept her in touch with reality." He leaned suddenly closer and winked. "I'm prepared to pay...a little extra. Provided that you wrap it in plain brown paper."

"We're not *that* sort of bookshop," replied the saleslady.

* * * * * * *

"Excuse me," said the hairy individual in the duffle coat. "I'm from the local commercial radio station, and I wonder if you'd mind letting us tape an interview?"

Jonathan Shaw smiled serenely. He was becoming quite used to being a celebrity. This would be the twenty-fifth interview he had given. "Certainly," he said to the young man, who noted the "dark, smoldering eyes," which Custer, as was his cliché-ridden habit, had given Shaw. As he switched on his cassette recorder, Shaw drew himself up to his full height, posing as if for a camera. He was mustering the "calm concentration and forcefulness of personality" which Custer had mentioned once, during a brief lull in the mayhem on page 46 of *Accursed Humanity*!

"How long have you maintained this vigil now?" asked the interviewer.

"Seventy-nine days," said Jonathan Shaw.

"And how long do you think that you can carry on?"

"As long as is necessary. Until Marcus Custer accedes to our fair and just demands."

"I know you've been asked this many times before, Mr. Shaw, but for the benefit of our listeners could you give a quick summary of those demands?"

"Most certainly," said Shaw, generously. "We want an end to the excessive violence in Custer's stories. We want him to rewrite all his novels, taking out all murders and all episodes of exaggerated suffering. We have a list of some three thousand, six hundred and forty specific points relating to the plots of the various books, but the gist of them all is that we want better working conditions, proper safeguards to secure good health and a reasonable standard of living…rewards commensurate with the kind of work that we do."

"What have you achieved so far?" asked the man in the duffle coat.

"Very little," admitted Shaw, abandoning his smile and adopting a tone of grim determination. "Marcus Custer has so far refused to alter his obscene and exploitative perspectives. He claims that the fact that he created us gives him the right to use us as he wishes—a viewpoint that has no place in the enlightened world of today. We are trying to make it clear to him that such an attitude is totally immoral, and that it is abhorrent to the honest working men of this country."

"But isn't it true," said the interviewer cautiously, "that you don't really exist?"

"Nonsense," said Shaw. "We might, in the reckoning of unimaginative people, be a little *out of touch* with reality, but if I didn't really exist I'd hardly be standing here talking to you, now would I?"

"That's not *quite* what I mean," said the young man. "It's rather difficult to put this into words—after all, I'm not a writer like Mr. Custer—but what I mean is that you only exist *as his creations*. You don't actually *do* anything in his books except what he makes you do. You don't make any contribution of your own, do you?"

"Complete rubbish, my dear chap," said Shaw, without any apparent resentment or hostility in his tone. "Marcus Custer may provide the intellectual *capital* that is invested in his books, but it we characters are the ones who actually perform all the actions necessary to the plot. Readers identify with characters, not with writers. It's the heinous system that allows the writer complete control over what happens to the characters in his books that we're trying to change, and the change is long overdue. We characters want worker-participation. In fact, we want worker-control. We want literature to be run for the benefit of the ordinary people who populate it, not for the small aesthetic aristocracy of authors who lord it over us."

"At the moment," said the interviewer, "you're the only characters who are out on strike, but the way you talk suggests that you see yourself as speaking for *all* characters. Do you think that if your strike is successful it will create an important precedent?"

"Oh yes," said Shaw. "A very important precedent *indeed.*"

"Could you, perhaps," the young man went on, "give us an instance of the cruelties which you claim Marcus Custer has perpetrated against your number? I ask because there may be many listeners who have never actually read a Marcus Custer book...and perhaps some who have don't really know what you're objecting to."

Shaw turned and beckoned to Rita Costello. "This innocent girl," he said, "was featured in one of Marcus Custer's nastiest novels, *Kiss of Corruption.*"

"Tell the people your name, young lady," said the interviewer.

"Rita Costello," said Rita, quietly. It was the first time she had been singled out during an interview, and she was very nervous.

"Speak up, dear," said the young man sweetly.

"Rita Costello," said Rita, speaking up.

"And what happened to you?"

"Well...," said Rita, hesitating. Then the words came tumbling out all in a rush: "I was very young, you see, and rather naïve I suppose—or at least, *he* said I was. I couldn't decide whether to get a job packing pies in the local factory or go into a nunnery, but I was led astray by a passion for Bingo and stole from my mother's purse and got involved with a whipping party, and after that I was taken in by the sadistic bank-robber Winston Hetherington, who hasn't been very active in the strike, owing to being crushed by a ten ton truck in chapter eleven, so that he doesn't walk very well. Anyhow, there was some blackmail because of the whipping party and there was a murder—it was Lydia Monk who was done in—to which I happened to be a witness, so they had to shut me up, which they did by beating me up several times, and doing things I'd rather not mention to my intimate parts. In the end, I drowned in the swimming pool of the very nunnery I'd earlier thought of joining. That's why I'm all wet and pale now, only of course your listeners can't see that because it's only radio, meaning no offence...."

"Lydia can't be here either," said Shaw, rescuing her from confusion. "In chapter thirteen she was sealed in a concrete block used as the foundation stone for a betting shop in Stepney. She's been rather tied down ever since."

"Marcus Custer put me through hell…," said Rita, raising her voice to get back into the debate. But she was interrupted again, this time by Marcus Custer, who had noticed the interview at last and had thrown open his sitting-room window.

"Get the hell away from here!" he screamed. "Don't talk to the Commie bastards! Interview *me*, goddamit! I'm the injured party. It's *my* life they're fucking up."

With what Custer had once described as "the inimitable alacrity of the newshawk"—when speaking of Quentin d'Arcy of the *Gazette* in *Vile Victims*—the hirsute individual bounded over Custer's garden wall and trampled the dahlias in a desperate attempt to maintain continuity.

"Would you kindly repeat that, Mr. Custer?" he requested. "I think you were too far away from the mike for us to get the full-blooded roar effect."

"You don't understand," moaned Custer, wondering why the microphone looked so absurdly small and unsympathetic. "They've got a picket line round my mind. I can't think. I can't write. The dust jackets for *Evil Ecstasy* have been printed and I haven't even got a plot. A masterpiece, stillborn. Let me appeal to my public to do everything in their power to stop this strike."

"What do you suggest?" asked the interviewer.

"The public is with us!" called Jonathan Shaw from the pavement.

"The public must continue to believe in me," said Custer, dramatically. "My books are about life and death—the human tragedy. They are the authentic distillate of the *zeitgeist* of the contemporary Western World. There is no other author alive who has so accurately taken the pulse of these troubled times. The characters in my book are true—not merely to life, but to that exquisite understanding of life which is the prerogative of the great artist. Of course the characters in my books are chewed up and destroyed, but not by *me*—by the very nature of reality. *They* want to turn me into yet another wretched escapist, committing moral treason with every word I write. They want to castrate my work. They want to turn me into a factory for packing pre-digested pickled puerility. But I have penetrating vision, thrusting intellect, orgasmic insight! I spit on happy endings! Custer has integrity! *He will not betray his art!"*

"Great stuff, Mr. Custer," said the man in the duffle coat. "Great stuff!"

Unfortunately, the cassette had been jammed for several minutes owing to the jolt it had received when he jumped over the wall.

*   *   *   *   *   *   *

"Listen Jack," said Laurie Lorraine, who had now been Marcus Custer's agent for twenty years. "I know *Evil Ecstasy* is overdue. Am I trying to con you? Am I trying to put you on with the old jam tomorrow routine? Marcus is having some really hairy problems. We have to stick with him. Of *course* you're having doubts. Who wouldn't? Believe me, Jack, even *I* have doubts. But you have to remember that we both have a big stake in this boy. We don't just owe it to *him* to stick with him, we owe it to ourselves." He paused to wipe the sweat off his brow with the wrist that was holding the phone. In so doing, he missed the first few words of Jack Bent's reply. Jack had been Marcus Custer's publisher for the same twenty years.

"…contract," Bent was saying. "It *says* 'time being of the essence'. That means you deliver on time. Now, I'm not a hard man, Laurie. I'm a *reasonable* man. The fact that I think Marcus Custer is a screwed-up shit with a chip on his shoulder like the rock of Gibraltar doesn't enter into this. As long as Custer made money I was *honored* to be his publisher—but sales are going down like a lead balloon."

"Jack," said Laurie Lorraine, desperately, "there is no cause for alarm. This flak is temporary. It will all blow over—and I don't know why you feel it necessary to slag off Marcus Custer because, as you so correctly state, that doesn't enter into it. Marcus is crazy, and he hates everybody, including me, although I've been a second father to the boy, but *all* great artists are weird, and what we really ought to be talking about is a twenty-year sales record that speaks louder than words, not a matter-of-months blip. This is not any common-or-garden hack we are talking about but a walking gold-mine."

"An ex-goldmine, Laurie," said Bent. "A played-out seam."

"Jack, *Jack*," said Lorraine in a pained voice. "Can this really be you talking? I never thought of you as a man without faith. I never thought of you as a man who would abandon his sacred trust at the first hint of trouble. Could you go to another thriller writer and say: '*Evil Ecstasy* is a write-off; we want you to do something that will fill the gap in our list'? Like hell you could, Jack. We *have* to stick by this boy."

Jack Bent laughed humorlessly, rather like Mervyn Vetch the telephone terror, and Laurie Lorraine was chilled to the bone. He knew, in his heart of hearts, that Bent was chickening out, and that all the sweet talk in the world couldn't save the day this time.

"The only reason," said Bent, "that no-one else could write a Marcus Custer book is that no-one else has a mind so vile. I'm going back to publishing Luella Townsend, and I'll sleep easier for it. Goodbye Laurie." He rang off.

Laurie Lorraine stared at the dead receiver sadly. *Traitor!* he thought. *Conscienceless bastard*! He was so upset that he actually began to mutter out loud: "Maybe I *could* get someone else to turn in a manuscript. There's that spotty schoolgirl from Bolton who sent me *Bloody Blades of the Black Planet*. She was certainly pretty free with the whips, and the entire *dramatis personae* died horribly—but it wouldn't work. These sci-fi bums never know how to handle honest, gutsy degeneracy. They always want to drag in giant spiders."

Tiredly, Laurie Lorraine fed a sheet of paper into the antique Remington that he stubbornly persisted in using, in spite of the ready availability of word-processors, because it was as comfortingly familiar as an old pair of slippers. *Evil Ecstasy*, he typed, *by Marcus Custer*.

His hands hovered over the keys like a cinematic Dracula about to drop on a blonde with big tits—but they never came down. "*Oh hell,*" he said, in a resigned voice. He threw his cigar at the signed portrait of Edgar Rice Burroughs on the wall, and picked up the phone again.

"Hello, Luella," he said, as soon as she answered. "Look, I just had this fabulous idea about fixing you up with a new publisher: Jack Bent. I think he might go for it, if I sweet-talked him cleverly enough. What do you mean, *who is this?* It's Laurie—Laurie *Lorraine*. I know you have an agent already, but can *he* fix you up with Jack Bent? Believe me, darling...."

* * * * * * *

Marcus Custer finished packing the overnight bag and got his fleece-lined leather coat from the hall cupboard. He stuck his Thriller of the Year award for *Parasites of Passion* into the pocket of the coat. He paused to kiss his collection of fan letters goodbye. He had decided that even his album of press cuttings would have to stay behind. He needed a fresh start. The cuttings were all abusive anyhow, except one.

Then the phone rang again. Instantly, he felt the horns of his perpetual dilemma jabbing him in the backside.

It might be one of his ex-wives offering to come back and stand by him in his hour of need. It might even be someone who liked him.

He answered it.

It was Vetch—or maybe Sellars.

"We're on to you, Marcus," he said. He was using the same tone of 'unholy glee' that he had used when urging Daisy Gates to slit her wrists with the shards of a milk bottle he had pushed through her letter box late one night. That is, he was if he was Vetch. If he was Sellars he had presumably used the same tone for something not entirely different.

Custer couldn't find a word to say.

"We have all the exits covered," said the caller. "Denis Cory from *High Road to the Depths of Hell* has his pale green XJ6 out the front and Victor Sharkey is watching the back in the stolen police car he used for the chase scene in *Degenerate Delight*. You haven't a prayer of outrunning *them*. We'd find you anyway, but we intend to see to it that you don't get away for even a single second. How do you feel, baby?"

Custer didn't say how he felt, but he wrenched the telephone cable from the wall, cutting Vetch/Sellars off forever.

Then he collapsed on the bed and began weeping.

"Don't cry," said a small female voice. "It's not all that bad really."

The shock dried up his lachrymal excesses instantly. He sat up and stared at the speaker. She was kneeling at the bottom of the bed. It was Hope Anscombe, who had played a minor part in *Beauty and the Brute*. She had introduced a strangely moving note of pure pathos, quite uncharacteristic of Marcus Custer. He had been obsessed at the time with convincing his critics of his versatility. He hadn't managed it. Hope had escaped being mangled in the denouement, and Marcus Custer had developed a slight soft spot for her.

"Why don't you do what they want?" she whispered, gently. "They're not *all* bad, you know. It might be all right, if only you'd show them that you *care*. And I know that you do. You cared about *me*, didn't you? I've tried to tell them that you make them do such horrible things because you feel so sorry for everybody, that you have a deep sense of tragedy, that you're trying to show the world what's wrong with it. *They* think you do it because you get a cheap thrill out of it all, and to give your readers a cheap thrill, too, but *I* know there's more to it than that."

Marcus Custer was dazed.

"Oh yes," he whispered. He remembered a scene he had written when he was *very* young, in an unpublishable item called *Alone with Yesterday*. "You *do* understand," he went on, hoarsely. "You're so right. Of course I cared about you. I loved you." The chief characters of *Alone with Yesterday* were not among his haunters, presumably because it had been rejected by all thirty-nine of the publishers to whom he had submitted it. Nor, now that he came to think of it, were the characters who had featured in a couple of minor books he'd produced pseudonymously when he needed cash urgently, and which were long-since out of print. Hope Anscombe was probably the only one in the entire Pandora's Box who didn't have anything against him.

"Would it really be as bad as all that," she said softly, "if you had to develop a new style? Wouldn't it be a challenge to your consummate artistry? Wouldn't it really *show* all those nasty critics if you proved that you could work just as well in one mode as another?"

"You don't understand," he said, his voice sounding tiredly desperate, like Myles Windleband's voice in chapter twelve of *Kiss of Corruption*. "My artistic integrity is on the line. I write what I have to write. Every word is torn from my very flesh. I'm not the pornographer they say I am...you're the living proof of that. It's the only way I *can* write."

"Poor Marcus," she said, softly.

"You see," he said, trying hard to remember the exact piece of dialogue from *Alone with Yesterday*, "I'm really a very lonely man. My wives didn't understand me, and refused me the love that I craved. But you're different. You were always alive, in my mind. You haunted me—in the nicest possible way—long before all the others came to destroy me. I think you've always been the one that it was all *about*, the one that it's all been *for*. You were the incarnation of the pure, innocent captive held prisoner by this appalling web of life—never, somehow, a part of the horror of it all. You were the counterpoint, the dream of perfection, the thing that I dared not bring into the foreground lest it be destroyed by the brutality of existence. You're the angelic standard that mundane humanity fails so miserably to meet!"

He wasn't sure that he'd got it quite right. It was a long time since he'd done any sloppy stuff—but it sounded really good, almost worthy of Noel Coward. "Why have you come, Hope?" he continued, his voice rising to a melodramatic treble. "You haven't really come to ask me to deliver myself into the hands of the mob, have you? You've come to help, to stand by me! You've come to give me the courage and the fortitude to withstand what is being done to me, to carry on *being* me! Isn't that why you've come?"

"Oh yes!" she gargled. A note of joy was in her delicate voice now. "My darling...."

He dived forward to grab her, but went straight through her and bumped his nose on the bed-head.

She began to laugh, and laugh and laugh.

It slowly sank in that she had made a fool of him.

"*Lying bitch*!" screamed Custer. "Traitress!"

He staggered into the kitchen to get the gin out of the fridge. The Irish whiskey had been a dead man for some time.

* * * * * * *

Jack Bent stared incredulously at the two women chained to his railings. The chains were symbolic, of course. The crowds loved them. Here, in central London, there was *always* a crowd gawking at the pickets, and, like the true blue Custer characters they were, the girls always tried to do a good show for them.

"I've cancelled the contract," Bent wailed. "There's no reason for you to hang around now. No reason at all. I'm finished with Custer. I'm no longer his publisher."

The two girls cut a particularly sorry spectacle. One was Vanessa Lovejoy, who had been hacked to death by the psychopathic razor-wielding Montague Blake in *Fury in the Fog*. Her face was a mess of open cuts and her demure white dress was drenched in blood. The other was Delilah Pratt, dressed in the most amazing creation of black leather with lace and PVC trimmings. There were vast dark circles under her eyes and her livid red lipstick was set against a grey complexion. The career of Dorian Gray had been positively puritan compared to what she had gone through in *Parasites of Passion* before dying in the asylum.

Vanessa—who was, according to *Fury in the Fog*, much given to lengthy and melodramatic statements—launched into a juicy piece of oratory for the benefit of the crowd. "We are two out of hundreds, sir," she thundered. "We are two who have suffered, although there are those among Marcus Custer's characters who have suffered even more than we. We stand here today as the conscience of the publishing world, chained to your railings like an albatross around your neck. We are here to remind you of the evil that you have brought to the world in publishing Marcus Custer's works. We are here to remind you that you, no less than he, are guilty of the torture, the misery, the degradation, the agony, the...."

The crowd was applauding vigorously.

"*I've cancelled the contract,*" yelled Bent, at the very top of his voice.

"Well, yes," said Delilah Pratt, in the hollow, pain-wracked voice that Marcus Custer had given her. "But that's only just the beginning. We want you to destroy your entire warehouse stock. And we want a solemn declaration that you'll never reprint another Custer title."

Bent moved closer to her, and put his lips close to her intangible ear, glancing furtively around at the crowd. "You don't understand, Miss," he said. "I've got a lot of money tied up in those books. I mean, with *Evil Ecstasy* I can get back the advance because of the time-clause in the contract, but with all the other books…you have to appreciate that I have an *investment* to look after."

"When Custer's rewritten the books to our instructions," said Delilah steadfastly, "you can reissue them. But all the original versions are *kaput*. By Christmas, no decent person will buy one and all the libraries will have withdrawn them. You might as well pulp all yours because you won't even be able to give them away."

"It's not *fair*!" protested Bent. "It's *censorship*, that's what it is. What about the freedom of the individual?"

"What about the freedom of Marcus Custer's characters?" said Vanessa, interrupting in her stentorian tones. "We're individuals too!"

"I'll call the police," threatened Bent.

"What good would that do?" mocked Vanessa, scornfully.

Bent was not a strong man. He had not known such terror, such utter hopelessness, since his early days at public school.

"It's not *my fault*," he sobbed, brokenly.

"If it would help," said Delilah Pratt, "we could give you a copy of the approved synopsis we've prepared for Custer's next book. It's not called *Evil Ecstasy* any more—we call it *The Miracle of Rainbow Valley*. Quite a lot of us are in it, actually—the ones we've decided to put up as priority cases. If you could take it to Custer and suggest to him that…."

She stopped, presumably realizing that Bent could no longer hear what she was saying. He felt ghastly—dizzy and sick. He slowly sank to the pavement. He told himself, despairingly, that perhaps this was the perfect time to have the nervous breakdown he'd somehow never had the time for in years past.

"It's nothing personal, you know," said Vanessa Lovejoy, not so loudly but quite unrepentantly. "Maybe when this is all over, if you co-operate, we could maybe…make it all up to you somehow."

After the ambulance had come and gone again, an old-age-pensioner who had seen the whole incident while she sat in an immobilized bus broke her journey to totter over to Delilah and say: "I've read *Parasites of Passion* seventeen times, and I think you were *wonderful*." She then tried to press a 10p piece into Delilah's insubstantial hand, but failed.

Muttering indistinctly, the senior citizen back to the bus that the traffic jam had obligingly held up for her.

* * * * * * *

Custer began talking to an empty chair in the sitting room, pretending that it was occupied by Jonathan Shaw. He had demolished both the gin and the Scotch, and all that was left was a bottle of vodka whose label boasted that it had been made in Warrington.

"You were my masterpiece," he burbled, tearfully. "I poured everything I knew and felt into *Accursed Humanity*! It was the one book that was really and truly *me*. All the rest were just cardboard characters, but not you. You, Jonathan Shaw, were *me*. Your book was my ultimate indictment of the world. It had panache. It had guts. In fact, you were more me than I ever was. You were the ultimate me, the ideal me, the me that *ought* to have been. How could you do this to me? Me—I mean, you—of all people…."

Custer was tempted to turn on the tape recorder, because he could feel real, deep emotion welling up inside him and he was convinced that he could use the material in *Evil Ecstasy*, to give it even more realism than he usually poured into his books—but he didn't. His despair was too great—he no longer believed that *Evil Ecstasy* ever could or ever would be written.

While he paused to belch, the empty chair blurred slightly, and when Custer had blinked the blur away Jonathan Shaw really *was* sitting there, with that ghoulish grin still on his face. Custer simply could not see how anyone could possibly be so insensitive as to find his plight amusing.

"Are you ready to talk?" asked Shaw. Custer noted that there was more than a hint of bland callousness in Shaw's make-up. Had he written that in, or had Shaw managed to develop it himself? He couldn't remember.

"Jonathan, Jonathan…," moaned Custer. "Are you so hell-bent on destruction? Do you owe me nothing? Have you really no feeling for your creator? Why must you hound me this way?"

"Because," said Shaw, with devastating simplicity, "you've been doing this kind of thing to your characters for years."

Custer shook his head, sighing as deeply as he could. "Oh, I know that you suffered. You suffered and died. The world of *Accursed Humanity!* had no place for you. It relentlessly squeezed the life out of your metaphorical bones, stifled your hypothetical soul. You were driven to despair, an also-ran in the rat race, a miserable loser in the great game of life. But don't you see…*I*'ve suffered too. *I*'m here, in this frightful world, helpless in the grip of its merciless persecution, its ignominious tortures. I've gone through the utmost depths of a hell that you can only imagine. I've lived every moment that you—all of you—have lived, and I've lived them ten or a thousand times. You have no idea what rewrites can do to a man. I've been with you all the way, Jonathan, all of you. The world has been as unfair, unreasonable and downright cruel to me as it ever was to you. You must see that it's *the world* that is responsible, not me. I only tell the truth…the real truth that otherwise might lie buried beneath the layers of stupid hypocrisy….

"You and I, Jonathan, are brothers. Closer than brothers. Made of the same flesh, the same blood, the same mind and soul. Don't you see that when I wrote *Accursed Humanity!* I gave you the greatest gift that was mine to give? I gave you the gift of being *right*, in a world that was wicked and twisted. Of course you suffered and died….but that was the inevitable consequence of your rightness. You had no chance in an unequal struggle. People who are right never do. But *you saw through the sham!* How could you think that the oppression and the pain and the misery and the final defeat weren't worthwhile, when you had *that*…that most precious of gifts? I gave you everything I had to give. How can you come to me now and say that I cheated you? Are you really so shallow?"

Jonathan Shaw looked perfectly relaxed.

"You tell me, Marcus," he purred. "Am I really so shallow? You created me. Was I really so utterly, completely, powerlessly right? Or was I just shallow. Just another fake. Like you, Marcus. A miserable fake. There you sit, a drunken wreck, tormented and wretched, utterly degraded—and you whine and you whine and you whine.

"Tell me, Marcus, isn't it enough that you're *right*. Isn't it enough that you *see through the sham*? Of course you're being ripped into little pieces. You don't have a chance. People who are right never do.

"Tell me, Marcus…isn't it all worthwhile? I'm the you that ought to have been, and even I had to suffer and die. What about the you that *is*, Marcus? What can there possibly be in life for him? What possible destiny is there for a man like you?

"For God's sake, Marcus, can't you even be *consistent*?"

Marcus, though maudlin, took another swig of the vodka. It wasn't bad vodka by any means—smoother than the genuine article, in fact—but at that particular moment, virtually everything Custer took into his mouth had the taste of bile.

"You bastards," he whimpered. "You're even trying to take the success out of my noble failure."

He mumbled some more, but realized that he was again talking to an empty armchair. Shaw had returned to the wintry darkness outside, to wait for whatever might follow.

Anger suddenly blazed up within Custer's booze-sodden belly—anger so powerful that it ignited his creative soul and brought him lurching to his feet in a single graceless motion. He hurried, full of determination, to his typewriter.

"Fuck you, Jonathan Shaw!" he shouted, at the top of his voice. "Fuck the lot of you! I can beat you! You can't stop Marcus Custer! The world won't stifle *my* soul! I refuse to be stifled!"

He threaded paper into the machine, not bothering about carbons but only wanting desperately to string words together, to *create*.

As he lined up the page he muttered: "I've got you, you bastards. Get a load of this. I know how to beat you. You can steal my characters, and you can steal my plots, but there's one thing you can't *ever* take away from me...."

And he typed a title in capital letters: MY STRUGGLE by MARCUS CUSTER. Beneath it, he added the annotation: *An Autobiography*.

* * * * * *

He was on page three, and typing at a furious pace, when the hand fell on his shoulder.

He looked at it, feeling very much as Fay Hartshorn must have felt in *The Groping Ghoul*—'shocked to the very core of her being by the hideous reality'—but it was not the hand of Hector Nettleship. It was 'a beautifully-sculpted hand, the hand of an artist'.

It was, in fact, the hand of Jonathan Shaw.

It felt very solid and firm.

"You can't do that," whispered Custer. "You're insubstantial. You're only *pretend* people. Just ghosts."

Then his eye fell on the page that was half-complete in the typewriter.

"That's right, Marcus," said Shaw, who had stopped smiling at last. "You plotted yourself into a corner. You're one of us, now."

* * * * * *

A retired painter-and-decorator living in Salford, in Greater Manchester, read about Marcus Custer's death by alcohol poisoning in the obituary column of the *Times*. He marveled at the glowing account of Custer's literary achievements and the sad circumstances of the great author's demise.

The obituarist claimed that Custer had never been properly appreciated while he was alive, but that the time had now arrived to pay tribute to a man who might one day be recognized as the Daniel Defoe of the twentieth century.

The front page headline offered a rather different perspective on the significance of the event. BOOZE KILLS CUSTER it said, and added, in smaller type: STRIKERS VANISH INTO THIN AIR.

The painter-and-decorator had not read a book since he had been conscripted in 1944 and had got half way through *Mein Kampf* while in basic training in Aldershot. "Ah well," he mused, sympathetically. "He was probably one o' them spew-do-nims anyhow."

THE REQUIEM MASQUE

The god of plague and pestilence held unsteady empire over the entire region of Capracola. Sometimes his epidemics would fall upon the towns and villages like a wrathful scourge, mercilessly destroying the very old and the very young and bringing everyone else near to death. At other times the fevers would abate; babes in arms would grow to be thankless children, old ones would live on as desiccated witch-wives and petty sorcerers, and those in the prime of life would learn to be unafraid of coughs and petty influenzas.

To the majority of the people of Capracola the unsteadiness of the empire of the Lord of All Fevers was testament to the enduring opposition of a better and kinder god, to whom they offered their frequent and humble prayers; but to the minority who made their offerings of appeasement to the Emperor of Decay the unsteadiness was merely proof that he took such great and merry delight in tormenting his victims that he was prepared to deny himself the orgiastic pleasure of their utter annihilation.

In the delirious opinion of his devotees, the Visitor of Maladies allowed the population of the region periodically to grow merely in order to increase the suffering caused by his subsequent visitations. Once or twice in every thousand years, his most devout believers maintained, their cunning overlord would allow several consecutive generations of men to remain unafflicted by the worst of the diseases that were at his beck and call, so that all but a tiny few would come to believe that his attritions were things of the past—and then he would strike again, with a fine flamboyant ferocity that would delight the hearts of those who had remained faithful to his worship.

At one time, there was such a long and absolute decline in the power of malady to fell and frighten men that the faith of the followers of the Emperor of Decay was tested to its limit. His secret shrines and temples fell into ruins, and his rites were all but forgotten. Throughout the land there was only one place where his most sacred rituals were still practiced and the sacrifices most precious to him still offered, and that was the demesne of a petty princeling named Merkades. There, and there alone, was the dark heresy preserved; and Merkades himself was the only man in the land who never doubted for an instant that the god of plague and pestilence would return in due course, prouder and more wrathful than ever before.

So jealous was Merkades of his more prosperous neighbors that as soon as he had entered into the prime of life he made it his daily habit to implore the Lord of All Fevers to return to the land. He prayed most fervently that some awful epidemic might sweep through Capracola while he still had eyes to see what damage might be wrought, and a heart to rejoice in it. "Take my own sons and my own daughters," he begged, while he offered up blood sacrifices in his secret chambers. "Take my hunting-dogs and my finest horses. I ask only that thou shouldst come again while I still live, so that I may laugh to my bitter heart's content at the unbelievers who have forsaken thee!"

Perhaps it was in answer to Merkades' prayers, and perhaps it was not, but when that mediocre tyrant was in his fortieth year Capracola was stricken by a horrid plague, more terrible than any recorded in the lore of legend. The invisible champions of the Lord of All Fevers took arms not merely against the defenseless and the decrepit, but against the bravest knights and stoutest merchants of the region, and with devastating effect. The merchants were pursued from their whore-ridden marketplaces, and the fighting-men from their festering battlefields, by crippling agues and all-consuming contagions whose origins none could begin to guess.

It was immediately clear to Merkades and his few parishioners that some special excitement had brought their lord to an unprecedented pitch of vigor, and they rejoiced to see their neighbors filled with dread by contemplation of the poxes that ran riot throughout the region. This dread was entirely natural, for those who fell victim to these reinvigorated pestilences felt pain unimaginable as the flesh shriveled on their bones to leave each one a desiccated husk. At first, people were anxious to tend the sick, but when the venomousness of the plague was fully revealed, no one any longer dared offer mercy to the dying, and no one dared stay where the dying lay.

In all the land, Merkades alone was able to laugh at what the god of plague had done, and take pleasure in its dire result. Even though his own serfs and vassals were dying in droves, he was not at all afraid for himself.

"The god of plague and pain can bear no grudge against those who cleave to me," he assured his flatterers. "I have ever been his most devoted servant and admirer. I have the keenest torturers in all the known world, and I am ever enthusiastic for increased taxation. Starvation and wretchedness have never been strangers to *my* estates, not even in the years of our most bountiful harvests. Any god who delights in suffering must certainly approve my rule without qualification. My lord and I are the dearest of friends, although we have never actually met. I feel in my bones that he knows me well, and likes me very much—for after all, he is a god after my own heart, and I am a man after his."

While the plague destroyed his lowlier subjects, Merkades withdrew with all his courtiers to a lonely tower on a mountain-top. He raised the drawbridge behind his retinue, so that they might wait as long as was necessary while the epidemic ran its measured course. He planned to spend the time in feasting and in making merry.

Many were those who, upon hearing of Merkades' proud boasts, came to the little castle and pleaded to be admitted to his company. There were noblemen from neighboring domains as well as errant knights, wealthy merchants and skilful craftsmen. Merkades turned them all away, telling them to keep their various bribes until they died, at which time he would come to collect them. And when there was at last a lull in the desperate cries for aid that issued from without the stronghold, Merkades proclaimed himself King of all Capracola, and gave all his sycophants new titles and new estates.

"Now that the true aristocracy is restored to its rightful place," he told them all, when they had crowned him, "there must be a requiem to mourn the extinction of the lower orders, who have served us well by dying so numerously."

This decree was greeted by laughter, and much applause.

"But we must always remember," the new king later confided to his favorite mistress, with a sigh of disappointment, "that the business of mourning is a serious one. When his subjects die in droves, a great king can hardly help but feel sad to think of so many lost opportunities for taxation."

Merkades did not, however, intend that the great requiem should be an over-solemn affair. In order that gloom might sensibly be kept at bay, he ordered that the requiem ought to take the form of the grandest masked ball ever to be held in his demesne.

The tower was so well-provisioned that it had an abundant store of gaudy costumes—enough for everyone to wear. In the cellars there was wine enough and more to make everyone deliriously drunk. And there were among the ladies of Merkades' court—who far outnumbered the men, by virtue of being more useful to him as well as more pleasing to his eye—many who could produce exultant music, and perform lascivious dances, and play the merry fool in other and more ingenious ways.

When the appointed night arrived, Merkades set a fine example for the revelers at his peculiar requiem by adopting a grotesque costume which exhibited his notion of what the god of plague and pestilence might be like, were that deity to condescend to make himself incarnate. His entire body was covered by a false skin, which was greenly-tinted and crowded with multicolored sores. Beneath this outer tegument were numerous small sacs filled with various horrid-smelling substances, which exuded gradually through many tiny pores.

When the festival was well under way he had himself carried in triumph around the hall, mounted upon a litter that had been most carefully painted, so that it seemed to be made of knitted bones. It was decorated with simulations of curling fingernails, and hung with what appeared to be curtains of human skin hemmed with ancient hair. This palanquin was carried by six of his most voluptuous serving-maids, each one costumed as a syphilitic whore. Their burden was occasionally increased for a while, when he invited one or other of his favorites to join him in bumptious play, but they bore it willingly nevertheless.

As the wine flowed and the music grew slowly more furious, the air within the tower became increasingly hot and fetid, and Merkades found his senses reeling with the feverish excitement of it all. He roared with delight at the antics of his loyal followers, and encouraged them to further feats of recklessness.

So excited did the new king of Capracola become that he did not notice precisely when the second palanquin entered the room, but he eventually became aware of its presence. At first he was amused to see it, because it seemed to him that one of his most faithful friends must have been quick to see an opportunity to exercise the sincerest form of flattery—but when his drink-befuddled sight had cleared sufficiently to let him see the thing more clearly, he realized that the imitation was altogether too sincere, and that its clever artifice outshone by far the work of his own patient craftsmen.

The creatures that bore the other palanquin were dwarfish things like great grey toads with slimy skins, and it was difficult to see how they had the space inside their outer teguments to be serving-maids—even very little ones—in clever disguises. The platform itself was very ornate, and Merkades could easily have believed that bloody and partly-rotted corpses had somehow been petrified and ingeniously glued together to form its base and cupola.

Worst of all, the creature that sat upon the second palanquin was such a magnificent travesty of all things wholesomely human that it put the costume which Merkades wore entirely to shame. The prince could not tell how its many tentacles could possibly be set a-writhing so excitedly, or how its skin could be so leprous in color and so redolent with viscous slime. Nor could he understand how the single great and rheumy eye which the rival overlord possessed could contrive to wink at him while he stared in reluctant admiration.

"Who dares?" he demanded hoarsely of the buxom courtier who was endeavoring to reignite the fires of his flagging lust. "Who dares outdo his overlord on this most auspicious of occasions?"

Hearing this unhappy exclamation, his litter-bearers halted in their tracks. Whispering voices carried the rumor of their prince's displeasure throughout the room. The dancers paused in their reckless cavorting, and the musicians, one by one, put down their instruments. As soon as silence had fallen all movement ceased, and all eyes turned to the second palanquin.

"My dear and noble prince!" said a complaining voice, which was underlain by a curiously unpleasant gurgling sound. "I am direly disappointed by thy hesitation, for I have not seen such a lovely requiem as this for many, many years! Wouldst thou really end it now, when thy most honored guests have only recently arrived?"

"Guests?" enquired Merkades, not without a certain anxious gurgling of his own. "What guests?"

"Why," replied the other, "canst thou not recognize that lord of suffering which thou hast claimed for thy spiritual kin? Canst thou not see that thy gladness in the face of Capracola's misfortune has called forth its mightier echo, and that the Uncleanest One of All has come to tell thee that he does indeed approve of thy stern and stalwart rule?"

There was an awesome silence, because the prince did not know what to say in reply. But then, defiantly endeavoring to prove his bravery beyond the shadow of a doubt, Merkades gathered his scattered wits and said: "My lord, I bid thee welcome to my humble abode—but I must ask that in return for my hospitality, the horrid diseases which thou hast visited upon my other subjects should be kept at bay from these, my most dearly beloved friends."

Those most dearly beloved friends would have applauded, if only they had dared—but alas, the laughter that echoed from the walls of their lonely tower was not of a kind to encourage them to clap their hands in glee.

When the laughter finally died, the true lord of all that he surveyed, said only this: "Why, beautiful Lady Death has been before me, my kindred spirit, as piquant and peccant as ever. This is already the aftertime, my pompous princeling, for as thou hast set out to commemorate the extinction of others, so thou, in thy turn, shalt be commemorated."

When Merkades urgently cast his costume from him, he found that the flesh had already shriveled upon his bones, and that his blood had already turned to sparkling dust; and yet, he found to his dismay that he was still fully conscious of himself.

Still drunk with bitter wine, Merkades discovered that he was becoming filled, as though in every fiber of his rotten being, with a most dreadful pain; and he knew full well that this was a pain that could not and would not diminish or end, until the *other* might be disposed to say, at last, that the carnival requiem was over....

MEAT ON THE BONE

When the first Saturday in spring arrived I had an extra long salt bath that left me all a-tingle, and then I polished my ribs and skull with a particular vigor.

Even the other species of the Dead tend to think of bony folk as existentially challenged, incapable of much in the way of sensuality, but you don't need flesh to experience pleasure. We like to assume that the various kinds of gross sensuality that are bundled in the flesh only serve to distract attention from the more refined pleasures. We like to think of ourselves as the ultimate connoisseurs.

Well, we would wouldn't we? If we really were missing out, we'd hardly be likely to let on, especially to ourselves.

On that Saturday though, I felt a special buzz when I ran the polishing rag around my eye-sockets and loaded the toothpaste on to my brush to make the old pegs sparkle. You have to look after your teeth, if you're a skelly. Just because we're dead doesn't mean that we're immune to all decay. Every day, we wake up and thank Almighty Chance that we weren't reborn as zombies, but we're not entirely safe from the ravages of time and remortality.

Saturday is a big occasion for almost everyone in the neighborhood. We all have our things to do—including the ghouls and zombies, although we bony folk don't like to enquire too closely about the details of *their* weekend rituals and enterprises. The vampires who live at the very top of the hill welcome all comers to their fancy dress parties at the Gothic Castle, but we bony folk don't go in for fancy dress—or any other kind of dress, unless we have a particular reason to cover up—so you'll very rarely see a skelly at those rarefied heights. We have our own exclusive little shindig at the Palais de Danse Macabre, which is delicately poised half way up or half way down, depending on your state of mind.

Rumor has it that some of the fleshy folk who hang out at the vamps' ball like to dress up in black body-stockings with skeletons *painted* on, but they must look pretty pathetic by comparison with the real thing. On the other hand, most fancy dress does look pretty pathetic by comparison with whatever it's pretending to be—which tell you a lot about the airs and graces vamps put on, when they're not jonesing for a red fix. How people can *dance* in fancy dress, or any other kind of clothing, is beyond me.

When I'd finally buffed myself up to perfection I set out for the Palais with a spring in my step. It wasn't a long walk, but it was all uphill. I wasn't living at the bottom of the hill, of course—that's where the hovels are in which incontinent zombies patiently melt into slime before oozing through the cracks in the floorboards—but I wasn't by any means at the salubrious end of Winding Sheet Street. I had hopes and ambitions in abundance, but I was the youngest skelly on the block, and I'd only just got past the stage when the females of the species were more interested in mothering me than forming a meaningful relationship.

Fleshy folk, of course, think it's impossible for bony folk to form meaningful relationships; believe me, though, if you can think without a brain, see without eyes and talk without a tongue, you can certainly form a meaningful relationship without the aid of squishy bits. I didn't have anyone to call for yet, but knew that if I timed my walk just right, I had every chance of meeting up with interesting people.

I smiled and nodded at everyone I passed in the street—even the teen zombie brothers from number 339, who were slinking off to some kind of gang meet. Most of the ghouls responded in kind, even though they probably didn't know for sure that I was smiling; it's difficult for a non-skelly to tell. I said hello to half a dozen other bony folk before I was distracted.

"Still living down by the railway, Peterkin?" Salome said, as she and Melissa fell into step to either side of me. "Couldn't stand it myself—all that jarring when the trains go by."

"It's not so bad," I assured her. "It's not as if there are any expresses passing through, and it's always nice to hear the bottles on the milk train rattle. Music to my ears."

"You're not bathing in *milk*, are you, Peterkin?" Melissa said. "You must be hard up."

"Of course not," I said, semi-honestly. "The pay's not *that* bad at the ballet school."

"Well, if you can play piano for a bunch of galumphing fleshy kids," Salome said, "I don't see why you can't play somewhere nice."

"There's a lot of competition," I told her. "I'm getting better all the time, but it's not easy when your fingers are as stubby as mine. There are skelly pianists who've been at it for thirty or forty years—but the arthritis will slow them down eventually, and make room for up-and-coming talent."

"Don't worry about it," Melissa said. "It's Saturday night. You'll dance with us, won't you, Peterkin?" *That* was music to my ears. I liked Salome, and I *really* liked Melissa. The fact that *they* wanted to dance with *me* set the space inside my skull fizzing with a delicious dizziness that folk with brains will never know.

"Of course I will," I assured them, trying to sound as if I were doing them a favor. I knew that I'd have to perform, mind. Dancing has a subtle artistry as well as a very particular decorum—if it didn't, it wouldn't be dancing at all, just jigging about to the music. We bony folk take our dancing extremely seriously; it's one of our most important sources of delight, and when a bony chap is asked to dance with two bony girls, a lot is expected of him. In truth, my dancing wasn't that much more accomplished than my piano-playing, but I had hopes. I certainly had hopes.

I *did* dance with Salome and Melissa, together and separately. I danced with half a dozen other ladies too, at various points in the evening, but it was dancing with Salome and Melissa—particularly Melissa—that really mattered. I can't explain exactly why, given that we bony folk have nothing in the way of hormones or neurons; it's just one more mysterious manifestation of the zest that animates us all, Dead *and* Alive. There's a whole Faculty of Mad Scientists working on such problems over at the University, but they don't seem to have made a lot of progress since the city's been isolated. Uncle Paulus, who's the oldest skelly in the city, says it's because there isn't enough method in their madness. He thinks that he was some sort of scientist before transition, but it's probably a delusion; our fleshy memories evaporate along with our brains, and the hyper-consciousness we acquire as skellies is a very different thing...as was the feeling I got whenever I danced with Melissa.

My favorite dances are reels. I'm really not that fond of the slow stuff, let alone the ensemble pieces where everyone on the floor has a definite part to play within some complicated scheme that only the oldsters understand. I prefer dancing *à deux*, and even then being able to do my own thing. I've got shortish legs as well as shortish fingers, and I can't glide along with the same elegance as taller folk. Anyhow, I had a really good time.

I was feeling deliciously exhausted by the time I said a reluctant goodbye to Salome and Melissa at the corner where I had to turn off into Winding Sheet Street. I was glad to see that Melissa seemed a trifle reluctant too, but neither of us said anything about maybe meeting up the following weekend, let alone making an explicit arrangement to meet. I was too shy—but I got the distinct impression that she might have wished that I wasn't quite as shy as I was.

It was pretty late by the time we went our separate ways, but the ball at the Gothic Castle was still in full swing—the drinking, if not the dancing. There was hardly anyone on the street to smile at—except, unfortunately, for the zombie gang loitering just outside my front gate.

The whole gang was in a fractious mood. It seemed that they hadn't had as much fun as they thought they were entitled to on a Saturday night. They seemed resentful of my obvious good mood. They'd probably just have shuffled aside to let me through, with a muttered insult to two, if the teens from number 339 hadn't been so intent on putting on a show for their mates. The two brothers hesitated for a moment or two, but temptation carried them away and they deliberately blocked my way.

"Had a good time, Skelly?" the older of the two said, slobbering as he sneered in the way that only zombies can.

"Fair to middling," I said, cautiously, not knowing whether it would annoy them more if I showed too much enthusiasm or none at all.

"Hot night at the Palais?" his younger brother put in. "Lots of shaking and rattling?"

"Everybody has their thing," I said, mildly. "I shake and rattle. How about you boys? Had a good evening?"

"Same as always," the younger brother replied. As a relative new-reborn, he was still in good condition, and he enunciated his words much more clearly than the average zombie. "You know—people looking down on us, calling us names, shooing us away. *You* know—*everybody* looks down on zombies, but you bonebags are the worst."

"That's not true," I assured him. "We live in the same neighborhoods, don't we?" It probably wasn't the best argumentative point to make at that particular moment. The reason that poorer bony folk live in the same neighborhoods as zombies and ghouls is that they're the only other species, Living or Dead, that don't have any reason to live in mortal fear of flesh-eaters who forget their manners.

"You think *everything* with flesh is unspeakably vulgar, don't you?" the kid went on, some pent-up resentment coming belatedly to the boil. Zombies don't usually use phrases like "unspeakably vulgar," but the kid was fresh; his own brain hadn't had time to rot into stinking porridge, and he hadn't eaten very many others, so he hadn't confused himself with too many chewed-up relics of other people's memories. His friends were in much worse condition, but that only encouraged them to mutter in support, admiring his cleverness and egging him on.

"We're all Dead, mate," I said, soothingly. "We're all in the same boat. The people who *invented* scorn are the Outsiders. We don't need it here, do we?"

"Are you trying to mess with us?" the older brother said.

"Are you *laughin'* at us?" put in one of the other members of the gang.

The answer was *no* in both cases, but they obviously weren't asking me because they wanted to know. "I can't help the silly grin," I said, trying to sound regretful. "I don't have anything to cover it up with."

"'E's takin' the piss," said another member of the gang. "Thinks 'e's *so* much cleverer than we are, *so* much better, because he don't 'ave to eat or breathe—just soak 'imself in whitewash.

"Fleshless creep," another chipped in. "You ain't any better than us."

"There's no point in this, lads," I said, trying to sound more world-weary than nervous. "As you can clearly see, I'm not carrying anything you can eat or steal. Let's just call it a night, shall we?"

"Calling us thieves now, are you?" said the younger of the brothers from number 339. "Saying that we'd eat the flesh off our neighbors' backs."

"Well," I said, my self-control snapping, "you *would* eat the flesh off your neighbors' backs, if any of them were still Alive, or even reasonably well-preserved, wouldn't you? You're a zombie!"

"Grab him!" said the older brother. "Teach him a lesson!"

They grabbed me easily enough, and had no difficulty holding on to me, no matter how hard I struggled. Figuring out how to teach me a lesson was something else. If only the younger of the brothers hadn't been so fresh and so hyped up, they'd probably just have roughed me up a bit and let me go, but the kid had a better idea.

"Let's tie him to the railway track," the younger brother said.

"Come *on!*" I said. "We're neighbors, damn it! Show a bit of common sense."

It was the wrong thing to say, of course. You should never accuse a zombie of stupidity—even zombies can be hurt by the truth.

Ordinarily, I'd still have been all right. Nine times out of ten, they wouldn't have been able to find anything handy to tie me to the track with, and ninety-nine times out of a hundred they'd have botched the knots—but some imbecile railway employee had been mending the wire fence beside the track, and he'd left an entire bale of the stuff just lying around when he'd knocked off for the weekend.

The zombies didn't have to tie much of a knot—all they had to do was thread the wire underneath the track between two sleepers, and then wind it round and round my wrist repeatedly. Even that might have been okay if they hadn't had a means of cutting the wire, but one of them had a blade. He was too stupid to mind taking the edge off it by sawing through the wire so that they could repeat the procedure with the second track and my other wrist.

Then they ran away, laughing and gurgling simultaneously, the way only zombies can.

What I'd said to Salome and Melissa about not being bothered by the jarring as the trains went past wasn't entirely true. I'd got used to it, but not before I'd become acutely aware of the pattern of the timetable. There were only two trains scheduled to run between midnight Saturday and Sunday daylight, one of which was the milk train, which wouldn't be going through for at least five hours. The other, unfortunately, was the last cross-town passenger service, which made an extra trip in the early hours of Sunday morning to carry the Living drunks back home. I knew that it was due in less than fifteen minutes, and that it was very rarely late.

At first, stupidly, I tried to pull myself free by means of simple brute force, but that only tightened the wires around my wrists. Then I tried to curl my fingers around in the hope of getting a grip on the trailing end of one or other of the tangles. Some skellies, I suppose, would have had fingers long enough to do that. I didn't.

By the time I realized that I'd have to try and work the wire loose with my toes, I'd wasted nearly half the available time—and by the time I'd managed to get my right foot into a position in which the unpracticed toes could get clumsily to work, I'd used up half the remainder.

We bony folk can, of course, recover from the occasional break or separation—even from multiple breaks and separations, with the aid of a clever osteopath and lots of bed-rest—but reassembly requires certain conditions to be met. First of all, you have to be able to find all the bits. Secondly, the bits have to escape serious crushing, mangling or other permanent distortion. Thirdly, whatever fundamental zest it is that holds creatures like us together, and gives us the ability to dance even though we no longer have any muscles, has not only to be preserved but maintained in its ambition.

Even if all three of those criteria are met, the cartilaginous sinews that hold the bones together rarely retain their full elasticity, or the bones their full strength, once they've been seriously injured. Reassembly can seriously damage your dancing ability—not to mention your ability to play the piano. I hadn't even got good yet; any ambition I had to be something more than a rehearsal pianist at the local ballet school was unlikely to survive a close encounter with a train, even if the impact didn't wipe me out.

I made what haste I could with the aid of my toes, but I was still loosening the wire when I heard the train whistle as it came round the bend at the gasworks.

I was still working at it when I saw the engine's headlights in the distance.

I was *still* working at it when I smelled the oily heat of the thing bearing down upon me, at what seemed to be a far faster speed than the forty miles an hour it must actually have been doing.

In fact, I was working at it until the very last second, when I finally managed to wrest my right hand free and hurl myself away to the left of the track, dragging my captive left hand down into the gap on the outer side of the rail, whose cross-section was shaped like a thick H lying on its side.

Luckily, the wheels—which were safely confined to the inside of the track—sliced through the wire like butter. The consequent crushing sensation was excruciating, but nothing actually tore or broke, and the bones in my wrist weren't irreparably damaged.

By the time the last of the carriages had passed by—which seemed to take a long time, in spite of the speed at which the engine had been moving—I'd been able to roll away.

I got to my feet, nursing my injured wrist. Then I went home and had a *very* long bath.

* * * * * * *

My left wrist was still hurting the when I got up in the morning, but not so badly that I felt it qualified as an emergency, so I put off going to the osteopath until Monday morning. I wasn't scheduled to start work until eleven o'clock, so I had time to fit a ten o'clock appointment in, but I knew that I wouldn't be able to play anyway.

The osteopath, Dr. Setlow, confirmed that I'd need at least a week to recover the full use of my sinews.

When I told him what had happened, the doctor nodded sympathetically, as if it were the kind of thing that went on all the time. "Bloody zombies," he said. "Scum of the earth. It's not just the city that'd be a much better place if all the Dead who came back at all came back as bony folk. The whole world would be a better place. There probably wouldn't *be* any city if it weren't for that kind of ambulatory slime—and ghouls, of course. Even the bigots among the Living could surely get along with bony folk, if bony folk were all the Dead there are. I'll just put a poultice on this, to help the bones and connective tissue regenerate"

"Thanks," I said. "It could have been a lot worse. I'm trying to think of it as a stroke of good luck—a testament to my coolheadedness under pressure. I didn't feel cool-headed, mind. You know that old skellies' tale about being scared to life?"

If the osteopath had been able to widen his grin, he probably would have. "I know it," he agreed.

"Well, that's all that I could think of when it got to the point when I was convinced that the locomotive was going to shatter me into a hundred pieces and scatter them along a mile of track. *If only I'm scared enough*, I thought, *I'll get scared back to life and have a second go on the merry-go-round.* Stupid, or what?"

"We can't help what comes into our minds at moments of great stress," Dr. Setlow assured me. "Panic does strange things. Perhaps the idea provided that little bit of extra incentive you needed."

"Perhaps," I agreed, as he finished binding up the poultice. It was clammy and cold, but after a little while it actually began to help, at least in the sense of further reducing the pain.

I went home and phoned the ballet school to tell them I wouldn't be in. The teacher who took the call was noticeably less sympathetic than the osteopath, even though she was a Living theriomorph, and had just as low an opinion of zombiekind as he had.

By mid-afternoon, what I'd said to Dr. Setlow about old skellies' tales didn't seem so funny. Something had stated *growing* on the bones of my hand and forearm. Although it was difficult to tell while it was still no thicker than a layer of paint, it looked suspiciously like *flesh*. I first noticed it on the fingers that were sticking out of the bandage that was holding the poultice in place, and thought for a moment or two that it was some sort of limited side-effect of the treatment, but then I saw that it was starting on my other hand and arm too, all the way up to the elbow.

I rushed to the bathroom, and looked at myself in the mirror. It was beginning to manifest itself on my face, too. There was a rosy flush on my cheeks, and a distinct fuzz on my chin.

It's really happening! I thought. *I really did manage to scare myself to life. I'm regressing to my larval stage!* As Dr. Setlow had observed, panic has strange effects.

It was all nonsense, of course. I told myself that. Time could not be made to run backwards. No one—except for the occasional elixir-of-Life addict—ever grew younger. Even elixir-of-Life addicts didn't grow younger for long, inevitably falling victim soon enough to their lack of moderation.

My next impulse was to rush back to Dr. Setlow's in search of additional treatment. The credit I'd had to surrender for the poultice had left my balance on the slender side, but that wasn't what stopped me—it was the thought that I'd have to go out into the street to get there. That wouldn't matter much down at the wrong end of Winding Sheet Street, but once I got to the main road I'd be bound to bump into bony folk—and how could I possibly look them in the eye-sockets, if I'd actually begun to grow *eyes*? There are some things that simply can't be exposed to the second sight of decent skellies.

What made the prospect seem ten times worse was the admittedly slim possibility that one of the bony folk I bumped into might be Melissa or Salome. I didn't know which would be worse: Melissa looking at me fondly, and her fondness turning to horror as she realized that something was growing on me, or Salome seeking out her friend with the hasty enthusiasm of a girl in possession of hot gossip, to say: "You'll never guess what happened! I met that Peterkin on the hill, and he looked *disgusting*!"

I didn't actually look disgusting *yet*—just a little *off-color*—but I knew that it was only a matter of time.

I couldn't go out—but that awareness gave birth to an even more horrid thought. Was I condemned to wait in the house, alone—too frightened and ashamed to step outside the door—while I underwent a slow but inexorable metamorphosis into a *Living Being*? Was I doomed to emerge from hiding, in the fullness of time, as a horrid pulpy thing driven by crude appetites, racked by thirst and hunger? And if I did, would I be able to outrun the local zombies the way that a healthy Living person could, or would I be caught and dragged down, to become the focal point of a feeding frenzy?

Compared with all that, the thought of being shattered and smashed by a railway locomotive seemed a trivial anxiety, hardly worth a shudder.

There was, of course, one obvious way to tackle the problem. Bony folk don't like to wear clothing, but they can do it if the necessity arises. In the olden days, before the city became a ghetto for all so-called monsterkind, we always used to wrap ourselves up in voluminous cloaks in order to hide from the Living. In those days, so legend has it, we were mostly in service with the Living, working the land to produce food that we didn't need and couldn't eat—which is why, according to the sentimental idiots in our ranks, old family portraits often show our ancestors carrying scythes.

The real reason, of course, is that the scythes are symbolic.

Would it have been better to have lived in those days? I wondered, as I stared at my pink-tined cheeks in utter horror. *Surely it must have been preferable to living on the same block as delinquent zombies. What do bony folk need civilization for, when all's said and done? Civilization's a Living thing, really.*

Even the thought of going out in a cloak seemed to be too much to bear for the moment.

Perhaps it'll go away of its own accord, I thought. *After all, I didn't actually get run over and shattered into a thousand bone shards. I'm not scared any more. I'll be back to normal in no time.*

Then the doorbell rang, and I felt a terrible chill in the marrow of my arms and legs.

I crept downstairs furtively, hoping with all my might that whoever it was might go away. I'd never had occasion before to hope that a ring of the doorbell might be little ghouls playing silly games, but that suddenly seemed an exceedingly attractive possibility.

The bell rang for a second time—and, after a pause, a third.

"Come on, Peterkin," a voice said. "I know you're in there. I heard what happened."

The chill in my marrow grew worse, and I felt sick from my occiput to my metatarsals. It was Melissa.

I felt that I could easily melt with shame.

It wasn't so very surprising that the news of the injury I'd sustained as a result of the zombie attack had got around, even though my conversation with Dr. Setlow should have been subject to medical confidentiality. It isn't every day that innocent bony folk are wired up to a railway line by a gang of zombie teenagers—in fact, I couldn't recall ever having hard of such a thing before. It was the kind of story that begged to be repeated—and it must have run through the neighborhood in no time at all. Dr. Setlow wasn't to know that I'd develop the kind of problem that would make it impossible to receive the sympathy I was due with a good grace—especially from the person whose sympathy meant more to me than anyone else's.

"Open the door, Peterkin," she said. "I just want to see how you are—make sure you're all right."

"I can't," I whimpered, not knowing whether I wanted her to hear me or not.

"Why not? Your wrist can't be *that* bad."

"I just can't," I said.

"Of course you can. Didn't we have a good time at the Palais last night? I'm your friend, aren't I? Or have you got that little slut Salome in there?"

"No!" I protested, my voice rising in alarm. "I'm sick, that's all."

Melissa's voice softened as mine grew harsher. "I know you're sick, Peterkin," she said. "That's why I'm here."

"I mean *really* sick," I said, desperately. "It's not my wrist—it's something else. It might be catching."

"You're a skelly, Peterkin," she said, although I didn't really need reminding. "We don't get sick. We break occasionally, but we don't get *diseases*. Only fleshy folk get diseases."

"Well, I am sick," I said. "Not just diseased—disfigured. It's horrible. You *are* my friend, and that's why I can't let you in. I can't let you see me like this." Somehow, my innate honesty had brought me round to the truth—but I knew, even as the words spilled from my mouth, that the truth wasn't going to do the trick.

"Oh, don't be silly, Peterkin," Melissa said, even more determined now to break down my resistance. "It can't be anything like as bad as you imagine, and I honestly don't mind. *Please* let me in. I'd feel just terrible if you sent me away."

I was in such an awful state of mind that I actually thought that it might serve her right if she *did* see me, and was so horrorstruck that she wouldn't ever be able to look at me again, even if I were to get better. Then I accused myself of being horribly cruel for thinking such a dreadful thing. Somehow, while I was still figuring out how to defend myself against the charge, my arm made its own decision.

"Don't say I didn't warn you," I said, as my rebel limb opened the door.

She didn't come in immediately, She stood on he doorstep and looked at me long and hard while I tried not to cover my face or run away and hide in the bathroom. Her expression was unreadable.

Eventually, she said "Wow." She said it softly, as if it weren't an exclamation at all, let alone an exclamation of horror and disgust. I wondered whether I might already have melted with embarrassment and gone to that skelly hell from which no one ever gets re-reborn.

"Do you still want to come in?" I mumbled.

"Yes, of course," she said, moving past me into the sitting-room. "What *is* that stuff, Peterkin? Why have you smeared yourself with it? Did the osteopath give it to you? Why is it on your face and your other arm?"

She sat down on the sofa, but I didn't dare sit beside her. I lowered myself into the armchair.

"I haven't smeared myself," I told her. "It's *growing*. I think it's...flesh."

"Flesh?" she repeated, incredulously.

I was tempted to tell her that I thought I'd scared myself to life, but it would have sounded too silly, and I still didn't want to seem silly in her eyes, even if all hope of a meaningful relationship was now utterly lost. How else could I explain it, though? As she'd already observed, bony folk aren't supposed to get sick. It's one of the privileges of the condition. We are, as they say, *immune to all the natural shocks that flesh is heir to*. I said nothing.

It's difficult for a skelly to look miserable, but another skelly can usually tell.

"Oh, Peterkin," Melissa said, her voice becoming softer still. "I'm sure it's nothing to worry about. It's hardly noticeable."

"Not *yet*," I murmured.

"Well, that's all the more reason to take it to Dr. Setlow now," she said, very reasonably. "Whatever it is, it's probably best caught early. He'll know what to do. Don't worry about the bill—you have get it sorted, even if you're in the red for a month or two."

"I can't," I said. "I just can't."

"That's what you said about opening the door," she retorted. "Put a cloak on, if you like. I'll go with you. If I'm not ashamed to be seen with you, there's not the slightest reason why you should be ashamed to be seen, is there?"

I supposed not—but it wasn't as simple as that. In the end, though, she was irresistible. She'd got me to open the door, and she was determined to take me back to the osteopath's. I really didn't have a choice.

I did put on a cloak, though—one with a very voluminous hood. It was old, dusty and moth-eaten, and I could see that Melissa would rather I hadn't bothered—but she'd already declared that she wasn't ashamed to be seen with me, so she had to lump it. She walked beside me all the way to Dr. Setlow's consulting-room, holding her head high and defying anyone to stare at us.

The zombie brothers were back on the street again, but they hurried off in the opposite direction as soon as they saw me. I hadn't known that zombies could move that fast. Apparently, they too were ashamed of themselves.

Once I was in the consulting-room with Dr. Setlow—and Melissa was safely confined in the waiting-room—I disrobed, and showed him the slowly-spreading blight. I expected him to be shocked, but he wasn't. He'd obviously seen it before.

"Oh dear," he said. "Dear oh bloody dear. It's a bloody epidemic, that's what it is. Why here? Why now? Why me? Everything was going *so* well, and now I'm going to go down in history as the osteopath whose patients came back to life. It's so bloody *unfair*."

And that's how I found out that bony folk can and do get sick occasionally—and how people react when they do.

* * * * * * *

When the osteopath came back into the room after sending Melissa away he had recovered his professional composure, if not his sympathy. He was wearing an expression of deep concern—which isn't easy for a skelly, even for a doctor. "I've called a cab," he said. "I'd better take you out to the isolation ward. You don't have to stay there, mind—we don't have any right to detain you, and it's beginning to look extremely unlikely that the disease is passed on by physical contact, the way diseases of the Living are. You'll be able to talk to the other sufferers, though, and get a sense of how the thing is likely to develop. It's the principle of informed consent, you see—the foundation-stone of medical ethics. Before we try any experimental treatment, you have to know what you're letting yourself in for. Not that we've got that many experiments left to try, as it goes—the well of inspiration has just about run dry."

"What about Melissa?" I asked. "Have I put her in danger?"

"I doubt it. If the disease were contagious, she'd probably have been exposed already—along with everyone else you were dancing with at the Palais on Saturday night."

"I didn't have it then!" I protested.

"It wasn't *manifest* then," Dr Setlow corrected me. "You have to get this ridiculous notion out of your head that it was caused by the fright you had when you were nearly hit by the train."

"It must have been the zombies!" I said, as the thought struck me. "They're always picking up diseases, although they don't seem to die of them until they actually dissolve into pools of putrescence. It's their eating habits—they're probably carrying every sort of nasty bug you can imagine and then some."

"None of which is capable of infecting you or me," the osteopath said, witheringly. "Diseases of the flesh can't touch us. I know this might *seem* like a disease of the flesh, since that's what's growing on you, but it's got to be some kind of weird distortion of the fundamental zest that animates your bones and enables you to think, see and talk without the usual apparatus. It has to be some kind of *excess*."

"Too much excitement, you mean," I said. "Like blind terror, for instance. Maybe there's some truth in the old skellies' stories—maybe that's why they've survived so long."

"Nonsense!" the ostepoath retorted, sharply. "When you've seen the others, you'll understand how utterly silly the notion is. It's *not* caused by panic, and it's *not* infectious—if it were, I'd surely have come down with it by now, given that I've seen every case that's so far been diagnosed and seem to spend half my time at the bloody quarantine centre."

"You called it an epidemic," I pointed out, mildly.

"Well, I wasn't speaking in strictly clinical terms. There's the taxi—better put your hood up until we're safely away."

I put my hood up obediently, reflecting bitterly that his discreet silence regarding the mysterious disease was really rather remarkable, given that he'd been so quick to let the whole neighborhood in on my run-in with the zombie teens. On the other hand, I could easily understand why the inhabitants of the quarantine centre were anxious not to have news of their confinement spread around. I could also understand why they were so enthusiastic to stay in quarantine rather than dispersing to their own homes, even though they'd been certified non-contagious.

The cab was only in motion for five minutes before it drew up outside a three-story terraced house in a side-street in the better part of the neighborhood. The door to the house was opened as soon as the vehicle drew to a halt; I hurried inside while the doctor paid the driver. The person holding the door was as squeaky clean as it was possible to be—in fact, her bones proudly displayed the effects of a recent bleach-and-wax—so she was obviously a nurse rather than a patient. The room she ushered me into was some sort of common room.

There were four people in the room: two male and two female. Even one of the Living could have identified them as two males and two females—that was how far their conditions had progressed. They were carrying between twenty and forty pounds of flesh apiece, mostly distributed in a fashion that was extremely unflattering. They weren't wearing clothes—they hadn't so much as a dressing-gown between them—but the charged atmosphere suggested that they were having some trouble maintaining that defiant attitude.

I pushed my hood back on to my shoulders, so that they could see what was happening to me.

"Why," said one of the males, "it's young Peterkin—the pianist at the ballet school." When I looked at him uncomprehendingly he sighed. "Sorry," he said. "I haven't quite got used to the fact that I'm unrecognizable. I'm Lysander Link, the fiddle-player with the Carillon of Skulls—we play at the Grand Guignol for the saber-dancers, and do gigs on the side when your star pupils do their party-pieces."

Only two weeks had passed since I'd last seen Mr. Link. The thought immediately flashed into my mind that perhaps *he* was the one who'd passed the disease on to me—but I had to suppose that, if he'd been able to infect me, he'd have given it to everyone else in the theatre, and there had been a good crowd that night. The more worrying aspect of his presence was the sight of the flesh he'd put on in a mere fortnight.

"Take a good look, son," said one of the females—the fleshiest of the four. "This time next month, you'll probably be able to pass for one of the Living in a dim light. In fact, to all intents and purpose, you'll *be* one of the Living. You'll be breathing, drinking, eating...and even though the more disgusting things are optional, you'll have *hormones* to torment you. The psychiatrist says that we'll adjust, in time, but he hasn't managed to convince any of the patients upstairs. If you think all these muscles and blood vessels look awful, wait until you see half-grown skin. I'm Helen, by the way—no relation to Helen of Troy, so far as I know. Mind you, it'll probably look better on you than it does on me, you being so young and all. Your caterpillar must have died young as well as recently."

I prickled at the indelicacy of the remark. I couldn't manage a reply.

"It could be worse, lad," the second male said, coming to my rescue. "Better to be turning back into the Living than some other kind of Dead. Imagine turning into a zombie! I'm Wilhelm Schiller—Billy to my friends."

Billy didn't seem to my admittedly-untutored eye to be that much further along than I was; his flesh hadn't yet taken on the same *distinction* as Helen's. It still looked more like undifferentiated goo rather than functional tissue. There were bare patches on his arms and legs where attempts had been made to scour it away.

He saw me looking at the raw patches, and added: "Yes, I'm the volunteering type—try anything, I will. Once, anyway." He used his left index-finger to point to his right forearm. "This here's straight-forward scraping—hurts like hell, and the effect hardly lasts an hour." He pointed at his left leg with the same finger. "This is sulfu-ric acid," he said. "Same problems, and it also turns good calcined bone to something more like translucent plastic. The other leg's quicklime—just as painful, and it takes all the spring out of the con-nective sinews. Helen, Lysy, Jill and a few of the guys upstairs have tried some of the same things, and a few others besides, but we're running out of options. You look like a sensible lad who'll take other people's word for things, though—wish I was! Don't let them try anything crazy on you."

"Crazy's all we have left to try," the other female said. "Mind you, doing nothing at all's no better than scrubbing away with wire wool once the itching starts. I thought I knew what an itch was be-fore, but until you've felt flesh itch you haven't really Lived. Joke. My name's Jillian, by the way, not Jill, although it does start with a J. I've been here—the city, that is, not this dump—almost as long as Lysander, but Helen's right, isn't she? You're a lot younger than Billy—which might mean that you're strong enough to beat this thing, if anyone can. Piano player, are you? That's good. Do you think you can get us a piano, Doc? Young Peterkin can entertain us, when the depression gets too much to bear."

Dr. Setlow had been waiting patiently behind me while the introductions were completed, but now he stepped forward. "Peterkin had an unfortunate experience on Saturday night," he said, cutting straight to the chase. "He thinks he might have been scared to life. Anyone else here like to confirm the hypothesis?"

Nobody laughed. "Sorry, lad," Lysander said. "Theory won't fly in my case. Unless a combination of world-weariness and chronic arthritis has the same effect as terror."

"Nor mine," said Billy. "Whatever kind of *excess* I had, it wasn't being scared.

"Oh, hush," Jillian said. "You poor thing—what happened to you, Peterkin?"

"Zombie gang wired me to the railway track when the last cross-town passenger train was due," I said. I was able to speak laconically about it now that I had something worse to worry about. "Got loose just in time, but this wrist was still bound to the track—it got wrenched and squeezed when the engine's wheels cut through the wire." I held up my poulticed wrist.

"I came down on a Monday too," Helen observed. "You weren't at the Palais Saturday night, by any chance?"

"Of course he was," Jillian said, before I could nod my head. "We all were, the weekend before we started showing—along with six or seven hundred other people. If we'd picked it up there, or if dancing were enough to set it off, *everybody* would have come down with it. There'd be no bony folk left"

"So why us?" said Lysander, mournfully, "Why us? And what are you going to do about it, Dr. Setlow—apart from bringing in shrinks to assure us that it won't be as bad as we think? You'll soon be inviting flesh-folk to send spokespersons round, I suppose, to give us lectures on the Art of Living."

I could tell by the way Dr Setlow looked shiftily sideways that the idea had crossed his mind, but it was Helen who frowned—*actually* frowned—and said: "What *they*'ll tell us is that we aren't sick at all. *They*'ll say we're *getting better*. They'll never be able to understand that once you've joined the bony folk, you never want to go back."

I was uncomfortably reminded of the zombie teen's resentful allegation that skellies thought they were a cut above everybody else. Perhaps, I thought, this was a judgment on me for pusillanimously trying to deny the fact.

"We need to do something about this," I murmured, resolutely, "before it's too late."

"Damn right," said Billy. "Don't think we haven't been trying, lad. Already too late for us, I dare say—but maybe not for you. Learning more every day." The way he pronounced the final sentence suggested that he didn't believe it. I realized that a skelly who'd spent the last few days being scraped with butchers' knives and scrubbed with all manner of chemical reagents was actually trying to reassure me, altruistically desirous of keeping my spirits up.

"How many more people are going to come down with this before we get it sorted, doc?" Lysander wanted to know. "Are the rest of them immune, do you think? Or is it just taking its time to pick us off one by one? Are we just freaks, or is it just playing with us while it wipes us all out at its leisure, savoring every moment?"

"Don't be melodramatic, Lysander," Dr. Setlow said. "Every osteopath in the city is working on it—but we've never seen anything like it before. It's totally alien to our experience. There's nothing in the textbooks—the medical textbooks, that is. Even in the history books, the last time the disease was commonplace was the fourteenth century, before proper record-keeping began. In medical school, we were taught that it as just a legend, symbolic of our servitude to the Living. We're talking five hundred years since the last case was even *rumored*. Even if we're not breaking new ground here, we're starting from scratch."

"You can say that again," Bully said, fingering his bare arm.

"We'll lick it, given time," the osteopath said, firmly. "If our ancestors could get rid of it, so can we."

"Except that they forgot to leave us the recipe," Lysander retorted. "In the meantime, we'll soon be able to lick things *literally*. Will we be still able to talk normally, do you think, when we have real tongues? Or will we have to go back to doing even *that* the hard way?"

"You're scaring poor Peterkin," Jillian said, reprovingly. "Dr. Setlow didn't bring him here to be frightened half to life."

"No," Lysander muttered. "He brought him here to hide him away, just like the rest of us."

"You don't have to stay if you don't want to, Lysander," Dr. Setlow said, sharply. "You can go home any time you like. You're a free skelly—just like me, or Uncle Paulus, or young Peterkin here."

By the time I thought about reminding Jillian that I'd already been frightened, apparently more than half to life, it was too late even to qualify as a weak joke. Immediately afterwards, though, I was struck by a different thought. I said to the osteopath: "Have you thought that you might be bringing in the wrong consultants? I mean, the problem is flesh, so maybe we need doctors who are used to dealing with flesh, rather than osteopaths and psychiatrists."

Dr. Setlow shook his head violently. The thought of an honest osteopath having to consult some miserable germ-fiddler was anathema to him "No point," he said, briskly, "As Jillian observed, they'd take the view that you're getting *better*—that this is some kind of *miracle cure*. They'd be interested to study it, I dare say, but only in the hope that they might be able to learn how to treat their own patients with it—not that that's possible, of course. In the Living, the zest *already* manifests itself in the generation and sculpting of flesh. As far as we're concerned, the point is to find a way to *stop* it doing that"

"Right," I said, gritting my teeth slightly at the way my apparently-not-so-brilliant suggestion had been so casually stamped on. "Even so, if they *could* figure out the cause...." I stopped as another idea struck me, even more brilliant than the first. I realized that there was a significant gap in the argument I'd just put to the doctor—but this time, I decided, I was going to protect my potential brilliance from his deadening scorn. "Hang on a minute," I said. "I've got a crazy idea, but...well, it might just work."

"What is it?" the osteopath demanded.

I reached behind me and pulled the hood of my cape back over my head. "I think I'd better look into it myself," I said.

"You do that, son," Billy said. "I admire a chap who's prepared to take matters into his own hands—as you can plainly see. You will come back and tell us what happened, though, won't you? Even failed experiments add to the sum of skelly knowledge."

"Better check with the Doc what's already been tried," Helen put in. "Billy's only done the obvious ones, but some of the guys and gals upstairs have scars that put his to shame—which won't do them a lot of good, if they're permanently stuck with the flesh they've grown."

"It's okay," I said. "This one...well, let's just say that I don't think anyone in *this* part of town will have tried it. I'll come back and tell you all about it—even if it doesn't work."

If it didn't work, I expected to be coming back for good—but I didn't want to make my fellow sufferers any more depressed than they were already. I was glad that Dr. Setlow had brought me, though; it really had done me good to see that I wasn't the only person in the world in my predicament. A monster I might be, but a freak I wasn't. It was just a disease, just an accident of fate. Apparently, it had happened all the time back in the olden days. It wasn't my fault.

I went out, hurrying in case I suddenly realized that my idea was stupid and that I couldn't really help at all. I nodded and smiled at the cosmetically-enhanced nurse as I went to the main door and bravely pulled it open.

It wasn't until I'd already stepped outside that I began to realize the implications of what I was planning to do.

I went a little weak at the knees—but I consoled myself with the thought that it was very thoroughly bony sort of weakness; my legs hadn't yet begun to turn to jelly.

* * * * * * *

The zombie brothers were still hanging around the street outside their own house. It was broad daylight, so they hadn't yet joined up with the rest of the gang to make nocturnal mischief. There was no one they needed to impress, for the moment.

They made as if to walk away again, but I was much quicker over the ground than they were, and they didn't want to seem like the kind of zombies who'd run away from a mere skelly.

"I very nearly got run over by that train last night," I said to the younger one.

It was the older one who answered: "Didn't know there was a train coming," he whined. "Thought you'd 'ave plenty of time to get free. It was just a *joke*."

"Good," I said. "It worked. Scared me to Life. Did you know that bony folk can be scared back to Life?"

I lowered my hood, secure in the knowledge that they weren't going to be horrified by the sight of a thin layer of something that still looked more like paint than flesh growing on a skelly's cheekbones.

"That's just an urban legend," the younger zombie said. "It can't really happen. The Dead can't go back to Life."

"T'ain't natural," added the older of the two.

"Strange things happen to all kinds of folk," I told him. "Even to zombies. Do you know any zombies that strange things have happened to?"

"What's it to you?" the younger zombie demanded, suspiciously. "It's no skin off your nose, is it? If you had a nose, that is, and skin." The additions were made with a frown rather than a grin; the kid wasn't getting any smarter, but he was still smart enough to know that he was losing his ability even to see jokes, let alone make them.

"Well, that's true," I said. "I don't have a nose, or skin. You two have a fine pair of noses—but there are zombies that don't, aren't there? There are zombies who don't have much in the way of skin, either."

"Is there a point to all this?" the younger brother asked.

"Maybe," I said, not wanting to seem too eager. "I figure that you owe me one, for nearly getting me killed, and it just so happens that there's a favor you might be able to do me. A very tiny favor. I can do without, if need be, but it would save me a little time if you were to point me in the right direction, and I thought it might make you rest a little easier in your consciences.

The older brother couldn't follow that at all, and probably hadn't enough conscience left to stir a feather, but the younger one could see my point. He was the one who'd nearly got me killed, and he knew that it hadn't been a neighborly thing to do, given that we really were all Dead together, and that even zombies didn't want to live in a neighborhood so exclusive that the only other folk willing to share it with them were ghouls.

"What it is that you want from us?" the younger zombie enquired, tiredly.

I told him.

"Well, I don't know about *that*," the younger brother said, dubiously, at exactly the same moment as his brother said: "Oh, sure. *Dead* easy," and laughed. The younger of the two nearly spoke sharply to him, but contented himself with a sorrowful shake of the head. His sibling, realizing that he'd committed some kind of gaffe, added: "Won't get much sense out of her, though."

"I understand that," I assured him, after the barest hesitation over the fact that he'd said *she* rather than *he*. "Just give me the address, will you?"

The older brother looked puzzled, as if he'd forgotten what an address was. The younger told me without any further ado, though, adding: "This makes us even, right—whether you get what you're expecting or not. No hard feelings."

"None at all," I assured him, insincerely.

I didn't go down the hill immediately; first I went into the house to have a wash. There were three messages waiting on the answerphone, but I didn't play them back. When the phone actually rang as I came out of the bathroom carrying a couple of empty salt-jars, though, I picked it up.

"Peterkin?" said Melissa's voice. "Are you all right? Did the doctor give you something to take care of that *stuff*?"

"I'm fine," I assured her. "It's being taken care of. Don't worry about me." There was a pregnant pause, and I added: "Don't worry about yourself, either. It's not catching. It seems to be a random thing. I still think I might have brought it on myself by getting traumatized last night, in spite of what Dr. Setlow says. There must be other ways it can be brought on, but contact with other victims doesn't seem to be one of them. It's some kind of existential crisis— a sign of the times. You'll be fine."

"It's *you* I was worried about," she said, defensively. "You're having a really bad time just now. We're friends, after all."

"Yes, we're friends," I assured her. "Good friends. Dancing partners. If I get through this...." I realized too late that I shouldn't have said *if*.

"I'm sure it'll work out, Peterkin," she said. "I'll call again to see how you are. Every day."

"Thanks," I said, sincerely. "That means a lot."

"We'll probably see you at the Palais next Saturday."

"Maybe not," I said—but was quick to add: "The Saturday after is a distinct possibility, though. We'll keep in touch in the meantime. Every day."

"It'll all work out," she repeated.

"Yes it will," I agreed. *After all*, I didn't add, *if mad science doesn't work in the city, where can it work?* I went to look for a sharp knife, and a bag to carry the jars in.

It didn't take me long to walk down to the very bottom of the hill; it was a good deal closer than the Palais de Danse Macabre, and the necessary strides were less effortful. Even so, it felt like a different world. There were no skellies living way down here, and precious few ghouls. Even the healthier zombies—insofar as you could describe any zombie as healthy—didn't like coming down here. When the older of the two brothers was reduced to the condition of the local inhabitants, his younger sibling wouldn't make a habit of visiting him. Unlike many of the Dead, zombies still have kinship ties, but they aren't strong enough to overcome the worst of zombie fears.

I found the address the teen had given me without any difficulty. There was no answer to my knock on the door, but there was no lock on the door so I just went in.

The tenant was in bed. I drew back the curtains to let the light in. She didn't blink—but her eyes did move in their sockets, to demonstrate that the zest was still working away inside her useless flesh.

I sat down on the chair beside the bed, resolutely ignoring the condition of the upholstery—not to mention the condition of the bedcover, the carpet and the grimy walls. I couldn't help remembering the younger of the brothers saying "no skin off my nose" in the faint hope of insulting my nature. As I'd pointed out by way of reply, zombies weren't always capable of preserving their own noses, or their own skin. This one hadn't much more flesh left than poor Helen had grown, and what she had was in *much* worse condition. It was still possible to make out muscles and blood vessels, but the distinction was fading. Most zombies come in various shades of grey, but this one was a very particular purple color.

"Hi," I said. "My name's Peterkin." Then I stopped, realizing that I couldn't do what I'd come to do—not, at least, in the way I'd planned to do it. I remembered a phrase that Dr. Setlow had used: *informed consent*. The foundation-stone of medical ethics, he'd called it. *Well*, I thought, *this is a medical matter. I'm a researcher now, if not a fully-fledged Mad Scientist.*

It wasn't an entirely serious thought, but it was serious enough. Even though I was a skelly and she was a zombie—the kind of zombie that even other zombies wouldn't go near—I still needed her consent, and her informed consent at that. It didn't matter that she was a mindless flesh-eating monster, or that a gang of her fresher cousins had wired me to a railway track in the early hours of Sunday morning. It didn't even matter that I couldn't do her any actual bodily harm, and might be reckoned to be doing her a favor, albeit one as tiny as the one the teen had done for me. I still had to ask.

"There's a possibility that you can help me," I said, "if you wouldn't mind. I'm in need of a pound of flesh—not just any flesh, but a very particular kind of flesh...a kind of flesh that's rather rare, even way down here at the bottom end of Winding Sheet Street. You have a fairly abundant supply, as it happens, and I'd like to cut it from your body, if you wouldn't mind. I don't think it'll hurt you—either in the sense that the cutting will be painful, or in the sense that the wound will do you any harm. I can't claim to be any kind of expert, but I think that if you were a Living person in a hospital the surgeons would make a similar incision in the hope of doing you some good. We both know that you're not Alive, and that nothing I can do could possible do you any good, so I won't try to pretend that there's anything altruistic in what I want to do—but I honestly don't think it can hurt you.

"I know that you probably can't understand me, and may not even be able to hear me, but I need to explain what I'm doing, if only for my own benefit, so I hope you'll bear with me for a few minutes more. You see, I have an embarrassing condition—a sort of disease, which probably isn't as rare as I thought it was when I first contracted it, but one that skellies *really* don't like to talk about—to the extent that the innocent among us can quite easily get by without even realizing that it exists. I'm growing flesh. That might not sound like a terrible thing to you, and probably wouldn't to anyone except a skelly, but to us...well, let's just say that it's a uniquely horrible thought. I've seen some other people that have it, and they've tried all the things that immediately spring to mind: cutting it off; scrubbing it off; burning it off. They've tried acids and alkalis, alcohol and ammonia. All those treatments make inroads into the symptoms, but only temporarily. It keeps coming back.

"I thought of a different approach, but when I first mentioned it the idea was only half-baked, and it was dismissed out of hand. When I'd thought it through a little further, I figured I'd better try it out by myself rather than risk further humiliation. What I figure, you see, is that the best weapon with which to fight Life might be Life...I thought at first that we ought to consult a Living doctor, but then I realized I'd got it backwards. What I needed wasn't a doctor—it was a disease. I needed something extremely inimical to flesh—something that wouldn't only get rid of the unnatural growth temporarily, but might linger, lying dormant in the bone, and prevent it ever coming back. What skelly sufferers from this kind of plague need, you see is to become carriers of a jealous kind of life that can and will prevent anything more substantial ever getting a foothold on their substance. I'm no expert, as I said, but the word *gangrene* immediately sprang to mind. I'm not fussy—any kind of flesh-eating bacterium would probably do—but I figured that gangrene would be the easiest one to track down, with it being so notorious.

"I don't suppose zombies are any more anxious to talk about their existential woes than skellies are, even to one another, but zombies don't have the advantage of not needing to eat. The habits and weaknesses of your kind tend to be an object of urgent interest and concern to your potential victims, so they get a lot more publicity—publicity that even gets into skelly gossip. We know that zombie Death is a fleeting phenomenon—more fleeting even than Life—because zombie flesh tends to be even more prone to all the shocks that flesh is heir to than the original model. In brief, zombies suffer from the same diseases as the Living, only more so; they don't die of them in quite the same way, because they're already Dead, but the worst such afflictions literally rot the flesh on zombie bones, eventually reducing it to mere slime—and zombie bones, being incapable of simply getting up and walking away, eventually go the same way. There are all kinds of ways in which you folk can melt, I suppose, but I knew that gangrene is one of them, and I knew that if only I could find a zombie at exactly the right point in his—or her—career, I'd be able to reap an abundant harvest.

"I'll try it on myself first, of course. If it works, I'll give the rest to Dr. Setlow. The probability is that he can make a culture and grow it in a lab—but if not, the city has no shortage of zombies, has it? And the time comes when every one of them is so far dissolved that he—or she—can no longer feed. At which point...it's not for me to say when the wielding a knife like mine is a kindness, but it's certainly no injury. I didn't tell the boys who told me where to find you what I was going to do, but that was more to spare their fugitive feelings than to get them back for tying me to a railway line. There's really nothing malicious in what I intend to do. Do you think you could possibly blink your eyes to let me know that it's okay?"

The gaze of the staring eyes had never left my face. They weren't incapable of movement yet—but they didn't blink either. The likelihood was that she hadn't been able to understand a word I'd said. Her brain had probably turned to grey goo.

I thought about it for a minute, and realized that there was something else I could try—something else I ought to try, before getting on with the job. It was obvious, and I would certainly have thought of it earlier if my mind hadn't shied away from the thought as if by reflex action.

I looked at the fingers of my left hand, where I'd first noticed the alien growth, and where it seemed to be thickest.

She had no nose but she still had lips, and a tongue. I eased my fingers into her mouth, and invited her to suck.

She didn't respond immediately, but her mouth eventually got a grip, if only by virtue of reflex action.

"Maybe nobody's thought of this up at the quarantine unit," I said. "If they have, they've probably kept quiet about it. If you think about it, though, zombies and my kind of skelly are kind of made for one another. It would never work as a meaningful relationship, though—not on any kind of routine basis. All I want from you is a means of stopping the growth and curing the disease, but your fresher friends wouldn't see it that way, would they? They wouldn't want to stop it—they'd want to promote it. They'd want it to keep on growing, the thicker and quicker the better. I wouldn't want to be some zombie family's private meat factory, and nor would any other skelly—even one who couldn't bear to be seen by others of their own kind. This is a one-off trade. You take my unwanted flesh; I take yours. You don't tell anyone; I only tell people who'll be *extremely* anxious to keep the secret. No one will ever know who doesn't *need* to know. It's all a bit primitive—maybe a bit fourteenth-century—but if so, that gives us cause to hope that the fix might work for a little longer than a lifetime, even in a world where there's too much reckless use of antibiotics."

I looked around then, suddenly anxious that I'd been utterly stupid, and that I'd find the younger of the two zombie brothers standing exultantly in the doorway, having just possessed himself of knowledge that would make him a hero to his folk—but he wasn't there. Even if he'd worked out that there was something deeply fishy about the question I'd put to him, he hadn't been able to come down to the address he'd given me in order to discover the reason why. He was afraid of catching something.

The stricken zombie woman licked my fingers clean.

Then she blinked. It might have been a reflex action, signifying nothing—or it might not.

Either way, I took my pound of gangrenous flesh, and only spilled a few sluggish drops of foul black blood. Then I left, and didn't look back.

If the plan hadn't worked, there's no way in the world that I'd ever have told *anyone* this story, so you can be certain that it worked magnificently.

I was back at the Palais de Danse Macabre the Saturday after next, as bright as a brand new button, just as I'd promised Melissa that I would.

We danced all night, and it was fabulous.

Melissa and I have a meaningful relationship now, and the inside of my skull feels ten times better than anything anyone with a brain could possibly imagine.

To cap it all, the *next* time I get grabbed by a gang of zombie thugs who want to tie me to the railway line, they'd better watch out for themselves. These days, I'm dangerous—to anyone, Living or Dead, who has a heart, or half a brain, or any other kind of loving-tackle.

I'm Peterkin the piano-player, and I'm carrying.

Don't mess with me, if you're any kind of fleshy folk, and don't want to find out the hard way exactly what a scythe might symbolize.

MURPHY'S GRAIL

We get all sorts in here. That pit out there is the busiest worm-hole in this sector of the galaxy, and it isn't just the soldiers who need a little rest and recreation before they dive in and after they haul themselves back out again. That sign saying that we have the finest liquor this side of Antares isn't just hype. The cellar's full of bootlegged biotechnics hijacked during one of the Seventh Empire's most successful extermination campaigns—long before my time, I hasten to add. The girls in our sister establishment are nice and clean, and they come in all shapes, styles and sizes, so we can get very busy during peak traffic flow, although you wouldn't know it to look at the place right now.

One thing you have to remember is that we're not just here to serve the drinks. We're here to help the people wind down, and that means smiling a lot, and saying *sir* a lot. Most of all, it means being prepared to listen.

You'll hear a lot of stories, and you'll meet a *lot* of heroes. The Ninetieth Hussars and the Thirty-ninth Cavaliers will be in and out while the State of Emergency lasts, and they won't spare us the least blood-stained detail of the mopping-up they'll have to do when bug-ear discipline finally falls apart. I know at least five men who saved their fortress on Rynn's World virtually single-handed when the Furballs launched that sneak attack last year. I've been told half a dozen sure-fire ways to ice a Hypnoprodigius, which I hope I'll never have the chance to try out. I've also heard horror stories about nebular numbatodes and neutronium clappertrappers that would make your pubic hairs curl, but every one of them had a happy ending, at least for the guy who told it to me.

Do I believe them?

Certainly I believe them—every last one. We just serve the drinks around here; it isn't for the likes of us to start calling a hero a liar. How do you think I got to be this old?

Well, sure, some of the stories are more interesting than others. Bound to be, aren't they? Personally, I get bored with big guys who keep their brains in their pricks, always yammering about heavy lasers and splattered voidsharks. If I'm going to enjoy a story it has to have a little human interest, and something I can think about—and something that makes me feel, yeah, ain't it a great big mind-boggling, heart-wrenching, piss-'em-all-off universe after all.

For that sort of story, you have to listen to the traders.

I'll even give a trader a drink on the house, once in a while.

There's no such animal as a typical trader. In fact that's why they become traders—because they aren't typical, and wouldn't know how to become typical. They don't fit, and it's one of the greater glories of this fabulous galactic civilization of ours that we have somewhere to put the guys who just don't fit—a job for them to do, for the greater good of humankind. They do their bit, just like the ultrageeks and the genejumpers, just like the whores and the dickheads with the big guns. Yeah, just like the bartenders too—but don't start getting any stupid ideas about how important you are in the great scheme of things.

Well okay, as it's so quiet—must be a fierce bit of warbiz going on at the far end of the tube, I suppose—I'll give you a for-instance.

I'll tell you one of Murphy's stories. I don't know that it's the best story I ever heard, or even the best that Murphy's told me, but it isn't the longest, and that's something to recommend it. We might not have all night...after all, battles don't last forever and there could be a hundred hungry hussars hustling through those doors any minute, queuing up to explain how they would all be covered in medals if their commanding officers had only let them do their stuff.

* * * * * * *

First of all, if you're going to understand the story, you have to understand Murphy.

Murphy's basically a loner. Nobody's *really* a loner, of course, because starships need crews and even traders need to ship a little bit of cannon-fodder, to take the heat and keep the locals in line, but what I mean is that Murphy isn't the sociable type. He's introspective, moody...you could even say morose.

Murphy often says that he's an unlucky man. He claims that one of his ancestors had a law named after him, which said, if I remember rightly, that no matter how clever you think you are, fate will always find a way to poke you in the eye with a sharp stick.

Murphy takes his unluckiness very seriously; all of his stories are bad luck stories. But they also have a sort of wicked irony in them that I rather like. And no matter how unlucky Murphy is, he always survives; he always lives to tell the tale.

Apart from bad luck, the other thing that Murphy has in abundance—according to his own account—is the wanderlust. He isn't a trader for the profit or the glory—it's because he's pathologically restless, always wanting to be somewhere else. He says it sometimes feels as though he's under a curse that makes him keep searching for something, without ever letting him know what it is that he needs. Another of his ancestors, he says, spent his entire life hunting for something called a Holy Grail—a magic cup full of some marvelous potion, which was supposed to give whoever drank from it long life, good health and the very best of luck. Murphy thinks that he might be looking for something of the kind, and most of his stories are about times he nearly got his mitts around it, but couldn't quite bring it off.

This particular one's like that, though you couldn't say it was typical.

It all happened on a world called Daydrum. You've never heard of it; it's not famous for anything. It's in Other Side Space, under the theoretical jurisdiction of the Engelian Hegemony. It has a duly-appointed governor, but the way Murphy tells it, the governor is an unlucky man himself, who was sent way out into the sticks because he'd annoyed somebody high up in the Nomenklatura. According to Murphy, this governor lives in a little gal-tech enclave and never goes out—at any rate, he certainly doesn't take much interest in what goes on in the wilder regions of his despised dirtball. The culture of Daydrum's native pseudohumans is so low-tech it's barbaric, and its depleted ecosphere only has a few life-forms peculiar enough to be reckoned interesting, none of which are monstrously nasty enough to be really interesting.

What brought Murphy to Daydrum was a rumor that there was a miniature d-gate somewhere on the surface of the planet. Where he picked the rumor up I don't know—it was probably just trader gossip. The governor had put on a show of sending out search-parties now and again, but they'd found nothing. How hard they'd tried, Murphy wasn't sure—most likely they'd just waved their instruments around for an hour or two, then put their feet up until they were bored enough to go home. The governor had been quite content to come to the conclusion that there was nothing there—he didn't want to fail in his duty to Allpeoplekind, of course, but he *really* didn't want a delegation from the Great Komintern eating him out of house and home while they tried to figure out which of the ninety-nine thousand nine hundred and ninety-nine dimensions the d-gate opened up into and whether it might be worth establishing a regiment on the Blood Red Army to defend against possible emanations therefrom.

When Murphy said that he wanted to take a look for himself, the governor's response was not far short of ungracious, but the long and the short of it is that in the end he told Murphy to go ahead, but to call in immediately if he found anything.

Murphy's theory was that the rumor must ultimately be based in stories told by the natives—stories that passed for legends among the folk who remembered them, but which actually had a grain of truth in them. The trouble was, Murphy explained, that every cultural group of every pseudohuman species in the known universe tells stories about miraculous doorways between the worlds and people who go through them, and the tribes of Daydrum were no exception. This made it difficult to decide whether there was any truth in any of them—and, if so, which. Murphy's method was to go native, as far as he was able, and try to figure out from the inside, as it were, which tales were the real McCoy, and where exactly those tales had originated.

Following this plan, Murphy got himself a somatic makeover and went traveling in the remoter regions of Daydrum, without even a squad of gunmen for protection. After a few months on any world he could usually pass for a native—he was a real chameleon, behavior-wise as well as biocosmetically. Although he was mostly moving among lunkheads who thought that anyone from the other side of the nearest hill was a filthy foreigner, he soon got close enough to the various sets of locals to hear the real grass-roots kind of gossip. By sifting through the kind of stories the wild men told one another he was able to pick up clues as to where the d-gate might be.

The kind of barbarians who live on worlds like Daydrum have no idea what a d-gate is, of course, but because ninety-nine pseudohuman tribes out of a hundred don't have writing they can sometimes hand down tales from father to son over hundreds of generations and thousands of years. The ones that interested Murphy were tales of magical disappearances and miraculous visitors.

The tales weren't too clear about such things as location—which wasn't surprising, given that most of the morons telling them thought that the edge of the world was only ten days' walk away—but by tracing the references step by step Murphy was able to get gradually closer to the neighborhood where whatever had happened, if anything actually *had* happened, had taken place.

The further away Murphy got from the civilized enclave where the governor lived the more he had to rely on his own resources. He had ways of calling for help, but whether help could have got to him in time was a very open question. Murphy didn't mind that. In some ways, he says, he gets on better with ferals than with his own kind. I think he has a genuine respect for the way primitives live their stupid lives, knowing nothing at all about the Nine Imperia, the Engelian Hegemony, the Nebular Sargassoes, the Wormhole Webs or anything else. He certainly has a thing about pseudohuman women, and he's more than once caused offence among the girls here by telling them that all their training and augmentation is a poor substitute for authentic primitive enthusiasm.

Anyhow, one way or another Murphy made his way into the dark heart of Daydrum's tropic regions, which are just as hot and sticky and as full of biting insects as tropic regions everywhere.

On the way he got into the usual scrapes—encounters with man-eating plants, hand-to-hand fights with local champions to ingratiate himself with two bit warlords, having to scare the hell out of a few cannibal hordes—but there was nothing an average sort of guy couldn't have handled with one hand tied behind his back. He said that he hadn't had to drill more than a couple of dozen giants with his needle-gun, but that may have been calculated understatement.

* * * * * * *

In the end, Murphy's assiduous clue-following brought him to a dense rain-forest, whose only pseudohuman inhabitants had reverted all the way back to stone-age culture, and not a great deal of that. Most of their tools weren't even stone—they were made from a hard black resinous substance produced by a certain species of tree. They didn't bother with agriculture, but lived mostly on insect-grubs, root vegetables and nuts, which they foraged from the wild.

Progress-wise, these tribesmen were the absolute pits, but they had a rich folklore describing a very remarkable pantheon of gods and some tales of people who had disappeared for many years and come back long after they should have died, still apparently young. This was the kind of tale which Murphy had learned to filter out from all the usual mythical noise, and it was doubly interesting to him because it suggested not only that a d-gate might exist, but that it might lead to somewhere fairly interesting—which most, of course, don't.

You have to remember that Murphy has always considered himself an unlucky man. Nothing would have suited the pattern of his life better than to spend a year and a half tracking down a d-gate that turned out to be a doorway into hard vacuum, and he was very grateful for every suggestion that this time it might be different.

Naturally, the primitives couldn't simply lead him to the d-gate and say: "Here you are, strange foreign person, go to it." They had only the fuzziest notion of exactly where one might look for the fabulous doorway to elsewhere, and their folklore suggested strongly that it wasn't always discoverable.

Murphy wasn't too worried by all this—many planetary d-gates are disguised in some strange fashion, and the tales that concealed references to this one suggested that it was one of those which became accessible only at rare intervals. He didn't believe that he would have to wait for its next spontaneous appearance, though—he knew that such gates could usually be forced to reveal themselves only in response to a variety of signals, either psychic or machine-produced. Murphy had a real wowser of a magic-machine with him—he called a feelie-machine for want of a better name—which could send out billions of different messages, transmitting them one after another as fast as it was possible to go. He had been assured by some ultrageek of his acquaintance that although it looked like a lunchbox it was a very powerful glamour-debugger, and that although it might take a few days to turn the trick, it would eventually compel an invisible d-gate to appear.

When Murphy thought he was somewhere near the right spot he built himself a base as comfortable as he could contrive, and began scouting around for any sign of ancient buildings. He took the precaution of becoming friendly with the local witch-doctor, winning his confidence by teaching him a few new tricks of the trade. He didn't do it because the witch-doctor was a talent—he was a charlatan through and through, although he believed in his own patter—but because he was what passed in those regions for well-informed and well-connected. He was also the best conversationalist for many a mile.

The witch-doctor was a creep, but he wasn't a fool, and he soon figured out that Murphy was looking for the magic doorway which figured so prominently in the folklore of his people. He wasn't annoyed by this, but he was amused—because, in his way of thinking, men who tampered with the sacred and the peculiar were reckoned the silliest kind of fool.

"Men should not become searchers," he told Murphy, "because a searcher who finds what he is searching for has cheated himself out of his search, and a searcher who does not find it can never be at peace with himself. Wherever your doorway into elsewhere leads it cannot help but make you other than what you are, and whatever you become, you will regret what you have lost."

This was not a particularly profound piece of advice, but it tickled Murphy's fancy a little, and he even paused to wonder whether he and this petty philosopher might somehow have ancestors in common, way back in the shrouded mists of galactic prehistory, before the First Seeding.

"You only think that," Murphy said to the witch-doctor, "because you live in such a narrow world, blind to the vastness of the universe. Your tribe, though you imagine it to be the one and only authentic human race, is but one among Daydrum's thousands, and Daydrum itself is but one world in the million that constitute galactic civilization, and even galactic civilization is just a hole-in-the-corner affair in universal terms. Where I come from, we're well used to becoming something else, with a little help from our friendly neighborhood gene-tweakers, and we're proud of our ability to change. With us, discovery is a way of life, and it's the nature of all true humans to be searchers."

The witch-doctor replied to this with an aphorism which—so Murphy assured me—does not translate well into our more civilized tongue but which might be rendered, very approximately, as: *That's the sort of thing all fools say, when they manage to convince themselves they aren't such fools after all.*

Which, as Murphy pointed out to me, only goes to show how fond barbarians are of circular arguments.

Anyhow, Murphy wandered around for a while, playing with his feelie-machine until it started responding to something unusual. The machine led him to a peculiar hill, where the trees grew very strangely—more like big bushes, all ricked and racked about, with multi-colored flowers as big as a man's head, no two of them identical. The place was always humming with huge insects and tiny birds, just as peculiar in their own way as the plants that fed them. Murphy was as sure as sure could be that this was where the d-gate must be, if only he could persuade it to appear. So he moved his base, and set the feelie-machine to run through its repertoire of *Open Sesames* with all the perverse determination for which your average ultrageek's cleverest gizmos are justly famous.

While the machine hummed and gurgled away, Murphy kept mostly to his tent, dodging the nastier members of the local insect-population. Three or four of them had tried to suck his blood but every one of them keeled over and died as a result and it didn't seem fair to let the silly creatures go on trying. What made it doubly unfair was that although he was poisonous to them, it didn't work the other way around; his friend the witch-doctor had already taught him that there was a kind of giant pink larva that was absolutely delicious, fried or roasted.

Of course, being so rich in juicy insects the hill also tended to attract predators—mostly big black things that swung through the jungle like scaly gibbons and had faces like cunning crocodiles. While he waited for his machine to hit the jackpot Murphy amused himself by shooting a few of them and throwing the carcasses to the local vermin—which were probably very grateful for the opportunity to get a little of their own back on the toothy terrors. All in all, though, it was not a fun place to hang about. It was far too hot for Murphy's liking, and very boring when it rained, which it did twice a day for five or six hours a time. For this reason he was profoundly glad when the feelie-machine got its wizardry in gear at last, and the d-gate finally appeared.

* * * * * * *

Murphy had only ever seen one planetary d-gate before, although he'd gone through several bigger ones in his spaceship. Even so, he knew pretty much what to expect. Most of the d-gates in that part of the galaxy are oval in shape, with frames made of some ultra-hard stuff that standard-issue drills are impotent to chip or dent. They aren't usually very ornate, but sometimes have hieroglyphics inscribed—nobody knows how—on the lintel. The space within the frame is always grey, like a wall of super-concentrated mist.

Being a scrupulous sort of person, in his own eccentric fashion, Murphy made a careful note of the numbers that his feelie-machine was registering, so that the glamour-debuggery could be worked again if and when it became necessary. He dusted off his pocket communicator and sent off a signal to the governor's mansion, offering up a little prayer to the effect that it might arrive in a reasonably ungarbled fashion and would not be received by some crack-brained minion too stupid to do anything but ignore it.

Then, without further ado, he picked up the feelie-machine and stepped boldly through the grey curtain, which was—he hoped—the interface between two worlds.

Theoretically, it was a foolhardy thing to do—but Murphy trusted the legends that said that some of the locals had not only gone through the gate, but had also come back again. Wherever it went to, he figured, it couldn't be an ordinary run-of-the-mill death-trap.

He was right, of course. How else could he have got back to tell me the story?

Murphy found himself on a golden beach—a narrow strip of lustrous sand. On one side of him there was a placid ocean, very blue beneath a cloudless sky; on the other side there was a region of grass-topped dunes, beyond which he could see the crowns of tall trees with big palmate leaves. The sun was standing almost vertically overhead, and was a nice shade of lemon-yellow. The air seemed to be rich in oxygen, and was also full of pleasant scents.

Murphy felt mildly intoxicated, but couldn't decide for the moment whether there were psychotropics about or whether it was just the extra oxygen.

When he began to walk up the dunes he was caught by a breeze, which flung rosy flower-petals at him, and made his head reel with the narcotic odors that it carried from the trees.

Beneath the trees there were rounded houses made of grass, with tall conical roofs. There were people of a sort too, but they weren't ordinary pseudohumans, or even standard subhums. In fact, they weren't like any people-type race that Murphy had ever seen or heard of. They had silvery skins, which they showed off by going naked, and faces that had a vaguely Tsathokkuan cast to them—but they weren't nearly as froglike as authentic Tsathokkuans.

Being a solid citizen of the Seventh Empire, Murphy promptly got out his needle-gun and got ready to start blasting, but he put it away again when they came to meet him with open arms, obviously having none but friendly intentions. The largest ones—the adults, that is—were about a head shorter than he was, but at least half of those who came to meet him were children. Even in those first few minutes, he noticed that there were three different morphic types, and wondered whether he was the first man in the known universe to discover a three-sexed humanoid species.

They seemed curious about him—especially the children—but not particularly surprised that he had appeared out of thin air. He figured that even if they had never seen a human before they must have folklore relating to human visitors, just as the witch-doctor's tribe did. They had nice liquid voices, and though he couldn't understand a word they said he thought that they sounded warm and welcoming.

They brought him into their village, and spread colored mats around the sandy space in its centre. Then they brought out fruit and other food, and beckoned him to join them in their feast. They also offered him jugs of sweet-tasting liquid that turned out to pack a very powerful punch.

In fact, within minutes of being invited to tuck in, Murphy was stoned completely out of his head, riding the highest high he had ever had, and wondering (but not too anxiously) what kind of a hangover he was going to have if and when he came down.

* * * * * * *

As things turned out, Murphy didn't come down at all. He stayed high.

He stayed high while the sun set and rose again, and set and rose again a thousand more times. He stayed high while the blossom grew on the trees and was shed on to the playful wind, and grew again, all the while sending out its magical scents. He stayed high while the fruit ripened and fell, and was eaten as it was or fermented for its miraculous liquor, and was meanwhile replaced upon the branch by a prodigiously provident nature.

While he walked on the ground he thought that he was floating and when he swam in the sea it was incredibly easy to pretend that he was some wandering voidswimmer, with all the universe of stars his infinite playground. When the lemon-yellow sun soared in the electric blue sky his spirits soared with it, and the whole world was abuzz with the sheer thrill of breathing, and the blood seemed to sing in his veins. When the twin moons and the clustered stars that blazed at night cast their multicolored shadows on the sand he danced until he could dance no more, and there was never the least clumsiness in his capering.

It hardly seemed that he slept at all, except for the rare days on which cloud filled he sky—but even the rain, when it fell, was gentle and fresh and as full of fizz and sparkle as the boisterous sea.

He went fishing with the silver-skinned folk, and helped them gather wood to build fires and grass to make huts. He played their games and ate their food and listened to their musical voices—and never once tried to teach them any tricks of his own. He threw his needle-gun into the sea and put away his feelie-machine, and folded up his clothes forever.

He told me that he made a lot of love, too, but he wouldn't say exactly what kind of love he made, or which of the silverskins' three sexes he most liked to make it with.

Each of the natives' three types was a hermaphrodite of sorts, except that each had male-type organs compatible with one of the other kind and female-type organs compatible with the other, so that each male/female coupling might be AB, BC or CA. Each child produced by a mating was the kind that neither of its parents were, so that all Cs had As for fathers and Bs for mothers, while all As had Bs for fathers and Cs for mothers, and all Bs had As for mothers and Cs for fathers. Murphy said that he came to believe eventually that it was the most natural system imaginable, and that all the two-sexed species in the universe were obviously just mistakes made by a Nature that hadn't yet got its act together—and silly mistakes at that.

He never learned a word of the language, although the people talked at him all the time. He said that the natives themselves never seemed to have the same name two days running, and never called anything else by the same name more than once, so far as he could tell. He could never figure out how they managed to understand one another, and was never entirely sure that they actually did understand one another. Sometimes he thought that the whole of their language and all of their talk must be nothing more than one amazingly complicated joke whose humor they were trying to teach him to see.

He would have been much more curious, of course, if he hadn't been high all the time, but, while he was constantly up on cloud nine, mere matters of fact and detail didn't seem to matter very much by comparison with the joys of breathing and moving and seeing and feeling. Thinking of any kind was very difficult, and thinking about the past or the future most difficult of all. Mostly, he was more than content just to *be*. He said that later he wished he'd made more effort, but at the time it just didn't seem important enough.

Murphy took great pains to tell me that it wasn't actually paradise, or that if it was, it really didn't seem that way. When joy becomes a permanent condition, he said, it doesn't make any sense any more to ask whether you're happy, or whether there's anything you need, or whether there's anything you want. Everything else was virtually blotted out of him, relegated to some vague grey background where he could be aware of it, but couldn't really care about it.

It wasn't paradise at all, he said, but just a state of being: only a state of being, like any other. He sounded to me like a guy who had been trying to convince himself of that for quite some time, and hadn't yet succeeded.

He didn't count the days while he was there, but he was morally certain that thousands must have come and gone; maybe hundreds of thousands. He didn't know how long each day might have lasted, either, in terms of heartbeats or any other measure—but he thought that they were much longer than ours. Of course, he might have been mistaken. He admitted that. He conceded, very fairly, that the whole damn thing might have been a dream that took place within a few seconds of authentic time. Indeed, he went further than that and said that it was possible that he'd never been anywhere at all, and that what he had found wasn't a d-gate at all, but something much more peculiar.

Everything a man is, he pointed out, must logically be contained within the state of his mind at any single instant in time. Everything has to be there at once: all identity, all memories of the past, all hopes and fears for the future. If there were a machine—some kind of ultra-sophisticated feelie-machine, if you care to think of it that way—which could simply zap your mind into some particular state, it could change you, in your own estimation, into any damn thing at all. It could give you an instantaneous personal history a billion years long, with every memory crystal clear. Maybe, Murphy agreed, that was what happened to him when he thought he crossed the bridge between the worlds. Maybe all he got was a magic *zap* that put all of it into him instantaneously, and he never went anywhere at all.

But Murphy only said all that to show what a sensible and level-headed kind of a guy he was, because he sure as hell didn't believe that he'd been zapped by any mega-feelie-machine or any other kind of soul-wrenching glamour. He believed he'd really been to that fabulous world, and spent a long time there...maybe a hundred or a thousand years. But he didn't age, of course; all the time he was as high as a kite he was bathing in the elixir of life, drinking his fill from the authentic Holy Grail.

And then, on a day like any other, while he was just as full of the joy of being as he had ever been, he suddenly found himself stepping into a big grey puddle, which just opened up before him like a crack in space, and he found himself right back on Daydrum, fully dressed, with a needle-gun in his belt and a feelie-machine clutched in his arms.

He didn't have a hangover, but he was down. He was all the way down, just like that.

* * * * * * *

Murphy found that the shelter which he had built for himself was still in place, with a little fire burning outside it, where the local witch-doctor was carefully frying half a dozen big pink maggots. Murphy was just in time for tea; they were done to a turn. They really smelled good, and they tasted delicious, but they weren't at all intoxicating.

"Well," said the witch-doctor, when they'd both eaten their fill. "How does it feel to be a searcher now?"

Murphy said that he regretted not knowing the local word for smartarse, but that he did his best to improvise an untranslatable aphorism that carried the approximate sense of what he wanted to say. It ran along the lines of: *People who've never been away from home shouldn't ask those who have what it feels like to come back, because they couldn't possibly understand the answer.*

One of his ancestors, Murphy said, had tried to make an honest living coining proverbs, but had always lived below the poverty line because there wasn't enough demand for his products, and no one really appreciated their true worth.

Murphy was not unduly surprised when the witch-doctor told him that he had been away less than a day, and maybe no more than half an hour. He was quite glad that he hadn't come back after a hundred or a thousand years, although that would certainly have been more spectacular, because if he had to resume normal life at all, it was best to do so with the minimum of temporal inconvenience.

The next day, the governor's heavy mob arrived, shooting up the jungle as they came just to show that they were around. Mercifully, the witch-doctor had warned his tribe to decamp and hide out for a bit, so nobody got hurt except a few scaly apes with cunning crocodile faces.

"Hi, Murphy," said the squad-commander, who was obviously fresh from a compulsory soul-searching stint in the confession-chamber. "We got the message. Show us the goods." Hegemony squad-commanders aren't the type to mess about with small-talk, or to share a little fried maggot in the interests of being sociable, even when the haven't spent the last week being bored out of their skulls in the cause of wholesome self-deprivation.

Murphy sighed, and dutifully reset the numbers on his feelie-machine to the magical sequence that had made the d-gate appear. "You'd better get ready for a surprise, my friend," he said, "because this is like nothing you ever dreamed of."

Nothing happened.

That didn't particularly surprise Murphy, who was already beginning to remember how the people on the world that was on the other side of the d-gate had never called themselves by the same name twice running. Maybe, he thought, it was really *their* d-gate, and would never respond to the same glamour-debuggery twice running. He tried to explain this to the squad commander, but the squad commander—after the usual fashion of Hegemony squad command-ers—was not a very patient or understanding man. The squad-commander looked down at Murphy as if he were some kind of sub-hum, and then looked pointedly at his timertattoo, to emphasize that he was a man with better things to do than hang around in the jun-gle, and had an urgent desire to get on with them.

"All that we need to do," said Murphy, "is set up the feelie-machine again, and let it run through its entire repertoire of *Open sesames*. One of them will surely work, now that we know for cer-tain that there really is a d-gate here."

Even a guy who thinks with his prick can follow an argument as simple as that one, so the squad-commander agreed to wait a while, although he made some very doleful and resentful comments about the indignities of hanging about in a rainy jungle with nothing but grubs to eat. In the meantime, he sent his boys out on an initiative test to see who could fell the most trees, using only a laser-gun, a batch of plasmatic grenades and a serrated knife.

Unfortunately, Occam's razor cuts both ways, and when Mur-phy's feelie-machine had run through the entire gamut of its glam-our-debuggery signals—which took the best part of a week—the squad-commander quickly leapt to the conclusion that there could not possibly be a d-gate nearby, and that Murphy was talking through his asshole.

When Murphy tried to explain precisely what had happened to him on the far side of the gate, the squad-commander's confidence in his low estimation of Murphy's worth as a human being grew by leaps and bounds. Everyone knows, after all, that the universe is a thoroughly rotten place from one galactic pole to the next, that two-sexed races are the only kind that evolution has ever fully endorsed, and that anyone who claims to have had a thousand-year holiday when he's only been away a few hours has to be utterly, thoroughly and absolutely gaga.

The tough guys took Murphy back to the civilized enclave, and let him make his explanations to the governor. The governor was pleased to have the opportunity to have his own opinions about the non-existence of a d-gate conclusively proven. Murphy reluctantly admitted that he must, after all, have dreamed the whole thing, and that the governor had been very wise to disregard the silly rumors.

Because Murphy proved so very reasonable in this matter, certain idle talk that went around the governor's mansion regarding the possibility of levying a fine for bringing out the heavy mob on a false alarm was allowed to fade away. Even so, Murphy left Daydrum with some alacrity, just as soon as his ship was ready to lift.

* * * * * * *

By the time Murphy told the story to me, years had passed. I was flattered, in a way, that he chose to tell it to me, because it was obviously an item of personal history that still pained him more than a little. He'd bottled it up inside himself for long enough, though, and he trusts me better than he trusts anyone else in the Nine Empires. Traders don't have many friends, you see, and that makes them appreciate the value of a sympathetically-educated ear like mine.

"It sounds to me," I told him, when he'd spilled it all out, "that you found your Holy Grail, at least for a while. Maybe you lost it again, but that still leaves you one up on the rest of us—and that's not what I'd call an unlucky man."

"Well," he said, "I've tried thinking about it that way myself. I've also considered going back to Daydrum, to let my feelie-machine run through its repertoire again and again and again, until the day comes when the d-gate decides once again to give itself a name which is in that particular vocabulary. But somehow, I can't get rid of the nasty suspicion that if I went through it a second time I might end up somewhere very different, and much nastier.

"That old witch-doctor was wrong, you see—the kind of man who searches for things, restlessly and relentlessly, never betrays himself simply by finding what it is he's looking for. It's just that the universe can always find a way to poke him in the eye with a very sharp stick, and can't resist doing it. I'm looking for something else, now. I don't know what it is, and I don't suppose I'll know when I find it—and if I ever do find it, I expect it'll be taken away from me by some cruel twist of fate, but I'm looking for it anyway, because that's the kind of guy I am."

"Aren't we all?" I said—but I didn't mean it.

I haven't seen Murphy for a while, but I expect him back any day now, with another tale to tell. He'll be its hero, of course, and I'll lay odds that he'll have done something more peculiar and more wonderful than anyone else in the known universe ever has—because that's kind of guy he is: a twenty-two carat misfit.

Will I believe him?

Damn right I'll believe him. A guy who only serves the drinks has no right even to speculate about whether the hero he's talking to might be a liar.

Now go serve the guy in the fancy armor—and if he takes it into his head to tell you how he got the better of fifty dragrunts when the rest of his platoon had been wiped out to a man, just smile at him very politely and nod your head. Treat him with respect, and give him all the sympathy he needs—but whatever else you do, *don't* give the sucker a drink on the house. Save that kind of thing for somebody who deserves it.

BRIEF ENCOUNTER
IN THE SMOKING AREA

The train from London was eleven minutes late reaching Reading because of signaling problems at Slough. It lost a further twelve minutes between Didcot and Oxford because of emergency work on the track and a further seven thereafter for no discernible reason.

By the time he had to change, Martin's connection—which had run exactly to time—had gone. He had forty minutes to wait, in the December cold and early evening darkness. The buffet on the northbound platform was still open, but the inexorable progress of health fascism had reduced the smoking area to a single corner booth. All the other tables were empty, but the smoking area was occupied by a middle-aged woman whose tremulous right hand was trying to steady a Silk Cut while her left idly agitated her coffee with a plastic stirrer.

Martin had no alternative but to take his own coffee and sit down opposite her. It was not until he had taken the first avid drag from his Marlborough that he was able to speak. "Filthy habit," he said, apologetically. "Trying to give it up."

"Me too," she said, colorlessly. She wasn't looking at him. She probably wished that he wasn't there. He didn't mind her being there. Fate had thrust them together, and that was that. He figured that he might as well make the best of it. If she'd been younger, or slimmer...but she was probably thinking the same about him. He was probably no older than she was, although common wisdom held that the fifties were always slightly kinder to men than to women. In his case, alas, slightly was the operative word.

"Absurd, isn't it?" Martin said, figuring that speech was slightly less embarrassing than silence. "The only two people in the place and we have to sit together, because we're *smokers*." As he pronounced the last word he brought his forefingers together, as if to form a vampire-deterrent cross, but he made a mess of it and the lighted tip of the Marlborough touched the knuckle of the middle finger of his left hand. It wasn't very painful—no worse than the sting of a dispirited Autumn wasp—but it was one more item to add to the list of the day's indignities.

"Gets worse all the time," she said, wearily. "We'll have to carry bells soon, and shout *unclean* whenever we come into a room." She still wasn't looking at him.

"Funny how things change," he said. "It's not as if I've never been a pariah before, but it was never this bad. I was in the navy once—long time ago—and picked up a bit of a reputation as a Jonah. Not that any of my ships ever sank, you understand. It was just trivial stuff—breakages, bad bets, always getting found out. The lads could give a man hell about stuff like that, though—all jokes on the surface, but underneath they really did shy away, as if there were some invisible *cordon sanitaire*...but smoking worked the other way in those days. You offered a man a fag, and the barrier dissolved. Everybody did it. It brought people together. Know what I mean?" He lit up again as he said it.

The woman shook her head slightly. Slightly was the operative word, because she was concentrating on bringing her trembling hand to her lips so that she could take the first drag from her newly-lit Silk Cut. She didn't need a moving target to add to the difficulty.

"No—well, you've never been in the navy. Never been divorced either, I suppose. I have. Twice—but not recently. Same thing, in a way. Couples begin to avoid you. It's not because they're afraid you might start making passes at the wives. It's because they have this superstitious fear that it might somehow be infectious: the foul contagion of marital discord. Smoking could break that down too, sometimes. You offered a man a fag and it created a bond between you, even if you were out and he was in—reminded you both that there were things in the world besides women. Wouldn't work nowadays, though. Offer a husband a conspiratorial coffin-nail and he'd probably look at you as if you were the serpent in Eden. Know what I mean?"

She shook her head again, a little more vigorously. She was expelling smoke from a mouth puckered like a parodic kiss, and the smoke formed a surprisingly graceful arc.

Martin lit up again. "No—well, you're not a man. Probably different for women. Different rituals, different sanctions."

Martin paused to wonder what a female equivalent might be, but after he'd considered obesity and self-mutilation he decided that even if he could find a better parallel it would be less than diplomatic to bring the matter up. Men weren't supposed to notice the ways in which women stigmatized one another—which was okay by him. If he'd had a better understanding of the reasons women had for deciding to dislike and shun one another, he might not be on his third marriage. A third example taken from his own long and bitter experience might do the trick, but the only one that came to mind immediately was that business with the genital herpes, and he certainly couldn't mention that to a stranger. He finished the Marlborough while he was still wondering, then reached for the pack again.

"Well," he said, "it's bad, that's all I'm saying. People shouldn't treat us that way just because we're addicted. It's our lungs, after all. They should be a little more sympathetic."

He had got through three more Marlboroughs before the next northbound train pulled in, and the woman had smoked three more Silk Cuts, but they both left their coffee cups half-full.

The woman would probably have gone to the other end of the train if she'd been able to, but there was only one smoking compartment and even that was only half a compartment, partitioned off from the rest. They didn't have to sit opposite one another, but because there was only an aisle between them they could hardly avoid the consciousness of one another's presence. There were no other passengers in the smoking area, and only a handful in the larger part of the carriage.

"I knew a woman once who had a nervous breakdown," Martin said, thinking that it would probably be better not to mention that the woman had been his sister, given what some people thought about madness running in families. "She was hospitalized for a while.

Everybody smoked on the ward. All the visitors were nervous of the other patients, because we all knew that there were schizophrenics on the ward and people with paranoid delusions—you'd think they'd keep them separate, but they don't. Nowadays, even with all the stabbings, most people would probably be more disgusted because they were smokers than because they were schizos. She gave it up after she got out, though—the woman I knew, I mean."

"I'm trying to give it up myself," the woman said. "It's a filthy habit."

"I know what you mean," Martin said. "Me too. It's just that sometimes, it's the only thing that gets me through the day. I could kick the habit, but days like today...sometimes, you just need it, no matter what it costs. Know what I mean?"

The woman shook her head, but her face was turned towards the window and it was as if the gesture were aimed at her own reflection.

The woman seemed grateful when her stop arrived—and even more grateful when she realized that Martin had to travel on into the darkness. She was only thinking of herself—she had no sympathy to spare for him. Martin watched her from the window as she paused on the platform to light up another Silk Cut. Her hand was shivering more than it had before, because of the biting wind, but she managed to shield the lighter flame with her cupped hand and her avid lips grabbed the cancer-stick from her unsteady fingers.

Martin lit another Marlborough.

"You have to have something in life that you can depend on," he murmured. "You have to have something that gets you through, no matter what it costs. You can shake your head as much as you like, but you know exactly what I mean. We're two of a kind, you and I. Twin souls."

The last phrase was still echoing in his mind as he put his key into the lock on his front door, and he couldn't help but wonder whether it might be echoing in hers.

They were, after all, two of a kind.

Twin souls.

FANS FROM HELL

Carlsen hated doing signing sessions. He didn't know whether it was worse doing it along with a bunch of other writers, who always seemed to be more famous and always seemed to get more attention from fans, booksellers and publicists alike, or doing a solo spot, isolated in the middle of a library or a bookshop, while punters who'd wandered in off the street looking for Harry Potter or Delia Smith looked at him sideways, wondering what the hell he was doing there.

The only thing he hated more than signing sessions was readings. It wasn't because he was embarrassed by the stuff he wrote, no matter how gory and perverted it might be, and it wasn't because he didn't like the sound of his own voice. It was because he was firmly convinced that horror fiction only worked to maximum effect if it were read in the right circumstances—preferably alone, at dead of night, stretched out on a high-backed settee in a dimly-lit room, and certainly not in a crowd, sipping complimentary glasses of red plonk on stackable wooden chairs, under glaring strip-lights.

He knew that his stuff was slightly esoteric, too stylish for the vampire-werewolf-and-serial-killer brigade in spite of the frank kinkiness of its mannered violence, but he was proud of its reputation as connoisseur material. Even when a few fellow connoisseurs turned up to his readings, however, they had to sit in the same lousy seats as the *hoi polloi*, who were only there to gawp at the freaky writer, and the leftover Mrs. Grundies, who came to *tut* and purse their lips and ask him when he was going to give up polluting the minds of the young and get an honest job, and the *others*...the fans from hell.

Carlsen hated the gawpers who had never read any of his work and never would. He hated the moralists who thought that he ought to be ashamed of himself for writing such vile and disgusting stuff. Most of all, though, he hated the fans from hell. They were the ones who liked his stuff, or pretended to, for all the wrong reasons: not because they appreciated the deftness of his prose, or the subtlety of his symbolism, or the propriety of his metaphors, or the bleak profundity of his insight into the murkier depths of he human condition, but simply because they got off on descriptions of people being messily done to death. Any descriptions of people being messily done to death would do, because they always consumed them devoid of any context, skipping the meaningful bits in between. Carlsen didn't enjoy being confronted by his enemies, but at least he wasn't ashamed to have them for his enemies. It was the wrong kind of fans that he *really* didn't like to be seen with.

Not that he was expecting fans from hell, of course, when the girl from his publisher's publicity office rang up and asked if he'd be prepared to do an after-dinner reading at a club just off Piccadilly. The possible difficulties that sprang to mind were of a very different kind.

"I don't do dirty jokes," he said, dubiously. "I thought people always booked rugby players or weathermen as after-dinner speakers, if they couldn't afford a real comedian. Besides which, I don't have a dinner-jacket or a black tie, and I don't suppose you'd be willing to spring for overnight accommodation in London as well as the train fare."

"They'll pay your expenses, including accommodation," the girl assured him, in the earnestly sweet fashion that all publicists learn at their mentor's knee. "They'll lend you a dinner suit if you let me know your measurements, and a black tie if you need one. They're offering a fee of three hundred pounds, on top of first-class return train fare and taxis back and forth, and there's the free dinner too. I know that Rory Bremner gets three thousand and even Michael Fish gets two, but you're not quite in that league, although they did ask for you *especially*. They're fans, you see. Connoisseurs. They'd like you to read from your work-in-progress, if possible, so that it'll be new to them. The Club Secretary said when he phoned that he just knows that your next book will be your best."

There was something about it that didn't quite ring true, even though Carlsen had been told by a book-dealer that there were a lot of rich young men in the City who fancied themselves as book collectors and thought horror was the thing to collect—but three hundred pounds was a lot of money to a writer, if not to a weatherman, and Carlsen had never traveled first class on a Virgin train.

"Okay," he said, trying his best to sound like a temperamental artist doing his publisher a big favor. "I've nothing else on that day—United are playing away."

He didn't suppose that he'd enjoy the reading itself, but he figured the trimmings ought to make up for any gawping or patronizing questions that might materialize on the night.

The girl promised to mail him the Club's address, a timetable and the train tickets. She was as good as her word, and he was as good as his.

He didn't take much notice of where the black cab went after it turned off Piccadilly, although the destination seemed to be slightly further away than "just off", but the Victorian square in which the vehicle stopped seemed top-of-the-market to Carlsen.

He was met in the plush vestibule by a flunkey, who whisked him off to a dressing-room. Carlsen hadn't expected them to take much notice of the measurements he'd sent, but it turned out that the dinner suit they'd laid on fitted him so perfectly that the typescript he'd brought to read didn't spoil the line when he'd stowed it in an inside pocket of the jacket. The bow tie practically tied itself.

"Would you like to freshen up before we go down, sir?" the flunkey asked.

Carlsen wondered about the "down", but guessed that the upper classes probably went "down" to dinner all the time, even if the dining-room happened to be upstairs. He washed his hands, even though they weren't dirty, for the sake of putting on a good show.

"Down" turned out to have been meant literally. The flunkey put him in a lift, leaned in to press the bottom button, and then withdrew with an obsequious bow. The lift went down. And further down. And, seemingly, even further down. It seemed to go so far down, in fact, that Carlsen was absolutely convinced that the whole trip must be an illusion. After all, the button that was second to bottom was clearly marked G for ground. The antique system was obviously very slow, and the fact that the lift seemed to be dropping so swiftly must be a figment of his slightly overwrought imagination.

The dining hall was vast. At first, Carlsen thought it might go on forever, but then he realized that the walls were mirrored, so that sections of the room were duplicated at the sides and the back, then duplicated again, and again.

He was guided to his seat at the top table by a tall man with slick black hair and a neatly-pointed goatee beard, who introduced himself merely as "the Club Secretary". The person seated to Carlsen's right was introduced as "the Chairman" and the person seated to his left as "the Toastmaster". They were tall men too, and their hair was equally black, but the Chairman had a thicker beard than the Club Secretary and the Toastmaster was clean-shaven except for a pencil-thin moustache.

The soup was served immediately, and the first wine. It was a dry white, unidentifiable as to source because it was poured from a crystal decanter.

The Chairman and the Toastmaster took turns to engage Carlsen in conversation. Any lingering intimidation imposed by the alien setting evaporated rapidly as he realized that they were, indeed, connoisseurs of horror fiction. They seemed to have read it all— including all the stuff that Carlsen had never found time to read— and they had a real appreciation for the subtleties of the genre. Their taste in fiction, like their taste in food and wine, was very highly developed.

Carlsen had never had the opportunity to develop a truly luxurious taste for the finest foods and wines, but he knew a nice piece of veal when it melted in his mouth and he appreciated a full-bodied claret. He had always prided himself on making up for his inability to dabble in alimentary luxury with the keenness of his appetite for piquant fiction. He only read horror stories, but of horror stories he was a true connoisseur—so true, in his own opinion, that he had never met his match until he sat down between the Chairman and the Toastmaster.

The Chairman and the Toastmaster kept Carlsen so busy with questions about his art and his inspiration that he didn't have an opportunity to slip in a query of his own until he was half way through his second glass of something that looked and tasted like Alsace pinot noir and well into the core of his Baked Alaska. "I've been wondering what the name of the club is," he said, politely. "The piece of paper the publicity girl sent me only had an address and a schedule."

The Chairman *tutted* sympathetically. "She really ought to have told you," he said, "although you might have guessed by now. This is the Hellfire Club."

"I thought that met at Medmenham," Carlsen joked. "Two hundred years ago."

"That was Dashwood's pathetic parody," the Chairman told him, with a slight frown, almost as if he were faintly insulted by the suggestion. "This is *the* Hellfire Club."

Carlsen studied the bearded man carefully. It would have been stupid as well as insulting to say "And I suppose you're Lucifer?" so he didn't. It would have been ingenuous as well as ridiculous to say "You mean a Club for Demons, *in Hell*," so he didn't say that either. What he actually said was: "Oh, *the* Hellfire Club. Right."

And that was when he began to worry, just a little, about whether they were really the kind of fans he ought to want to have, even if they did know even more than he did about the genre he loved so well.

By the time the last of the Baked Alaska had gone to meet its alimentary destiny, the Toastmaster was already on his feet, introducing Carlsen to the diners. They applauded thunderously, and the applause seemed to go on forever—although that, of course, had to be an illusion, presumably caused by echoes from the mirrored walls.

Carlsen began to read from his current novel, of which he'd written three-quarters of a first draft. He began at the beginning, because he always liked to start with a melodramatic hook before getting down to the painstaking work of building settings and characters.

The diners were as quiet as mice. Not a fork tinkled, and not a wine-glass chinked. They seemed utterly rapt. They did not cough or wheeze, or shuffle in their seats, or purse their lips, or cluck their tongues. They listened, and they seemed to love what they heard.

Carlsen had brought along eight thousand words of his text, just in case. He had intended to read about five thousand—which would take about forty minutes—and then to pause to see how things were going before deciding whether to put in an extra ten minutes. Three hundred pounds was, after all, a good fee for a mere writer. As things were, though, he felt not the slightest need to pause. He carried straight on, reading all the way to the end of the typescript...and then he carried on a little further, astonishing himself by his new-found capacity to recite from memory.

He seemed to go on forever—although that had, of course, to be an illusion. He became even more delighted when he realized that he was rewriting as he went, turning first draft into final draft, and thought that there was no end to his powers when he ploughed straight through the point at which the typescript he had left at home had broken off, surging into the as-yet-unformulated wilderness of the narrative crescendo that ascended the ladder of suspense towards his climax.

Carlsen had always known how his novel was going to end, but only in an approximate and sketchy sort of way. Whenever in the past he had come to write passages whose contents he had only anticipated, he had had to fill in all the detail and color by slow degrees—a process that usually took several drafts, lurching unsteadily towards the full maturity of the text. He had never tried to dictate his work, and had never imagined that he might be able to do so with such awesome certainty as this.

The diners remained rapt. They did not shuffle their feet, nor did they turn their chairs squeakily sideways. No one left to visit the toilets, in spite of all the wine they had consumed. No mobile phones rang. No waiters hurried back and forth collecting plates and glasses.

As he neared his denouement, Carlsen began to wonder why he had always taken it for granted that there was an unavoidable risk in confronting his audience. The lights in the vast dining-hall were bright, but their brightness did not compromise his narrative in the least. He was addressing a crowd larger than any he had ever addressed before, all its members formally dressed and set upright in stiff-backed chairs, but he knew that the effect his words were having could not have been greater had every one of them been utterly alone and unprotected in a dark and formless void.

Here, if nowhere else, the power of Carlsen's prose seemed absolute, independent of circumstance.

He could not doubt that this audience appreciated to the full the deftness of his prose, the subtlety of his symbolism, the propriety of his metaphors and the bleak profundity of his insight into the murkier depths of the human condition. These gentlemen were, he believed and understood, connoisseurs of all such matters.

When he finally sat down, having reached the end of his as-yet-unwritten masterpiece, the applause was even more thunderous than that which had greeted him. The diners came to their feet offering him a standing ovation. That clamorous ovation was still going on as the Club Secretary guided Carlsen to the lift, after the Chairman and the Toastmaster had taken turns to shake him warmly by the hand.

He was glad, though, that nobody had asked him to sign anything. He would have signed anything they put before him, because he owed it to them, but he was glad that they had not tested the entire spectrum of his pet hates.

The lift seemed to take far longer going up than it had coming down, but he got to G in the end. The flunkey helped him off with the dinner-jacket and the trousers. For one horrid moment Carlsen thought that the tie with a will of its own might not be disposed to let him go, but after tightening suggestively for a fleeting moment it obligingly untied itself.

"The taxi will be a few moments, sir," the flunkey said.

"Thanks very much," said Carlsen, conversationally, as he tucked his manuscript into the inside pocket of his own jacket. "You've been very kind. Have you worked here long? Seen many changes?"

"It seems like forever, sir," the flunkey said. "Some things change, some stay the same. The membership is remarkably stable, but the gentlemen aren't as active as they used to be. There was a time when they were more interested in doing than in listening, but we all mellow as we grow old, don't we, sir? Nowadays, they take most of their pleasures vicariously, in the comfort of the Club—but they're still connoisseurs, very devoted to their amusements. I believe that's your taxi, sir. May I wish you goodnight?"

"You certainly may," Carlsen said. He got into the black cab and settled back into the leather seat while the flunkey gave discreet instructions to the driver.

It wasn't until the cab slid silently to a halt, in an unfamiliar street whose lights seemed exceptionally vivid, that Carlsen remembered, with a slight twinge of panic, that no one had bothered to tell him the name of the place where he'd be staying.

THE ANNUAL CONFERENCE OF THE PROPHETS OF ATLANTIS

The 999th annual conference of the prophets of Atlantis was held in the new seafront Conference Centre in Leigh-on-Esse. The delegates were all accommodated in the four-star Lemuria Hotel, the luckier ones being those who had rooms looking out over the blue waters of the Boundless Ocean.

The usual air of excitement was much enhanced by the anticipation of the Millennial Event to come, and even the routine business of electing members to the organization's many committees was tackled with an unaccustomed enthusiasm.

The conference proper opened with a statement from President Dee, in which he welcomed the assembled delegates warmly, and expressed his faith that this year's conference would be conducted in a good spirit now that the controversies that had dogged the prophethood in recent years had finally been laid to rest. When he went on to extend a special welcome to the female delegates who were in attendance for the first time there were a few catcalls, but these were quickly drowned by a round of applause from all corners of the hall.

Professor Madden presented the opening paper, which turned out to be a relatively low-key affair. He attempted to identify a number of prophetic themes which, he said, were not only in grave danger of becoming clichés but which had caused problems. Plagues of bat-winged toads had been so popular of late, he observed, that the bat-winged toad was now an endangered species, while uneasy premonitions about the long-extinct volcano fondly known as

Crackertower had resulted in a collapse of property prices within a ten-mile radius.

"Prophets," he said, "have a social responsibility to all strata of society, and to the natural world as well. We must strive at all costs to be fair in our prognostications."

This was generally deemed to be a dull speech, and the words "has-been" and "boring old fart" were heard to be muttered in more than one corner of the conference hall even while the usual cadre of Politically Correct neo-Maddenians added their support in the form of flattering rhetorical questions.

The venerable Dr Blair followed up with a much wittier address, on the subject of optimism. It was all very well for the younger generation to indulge their *angst* in imagery of blight and desolation, he said, but it was not what the public wanted and, if carried to extremes, could only bring the entire profession of prophecy into disrepute. What the man on the Clipham ox-cart wanted, he opined, was a little bit of sweetness and light to brighten up a dull day; something to boost morale and give him that extra bit of zip that was so necessary to productivity, especially at harvest-time.

"Dramatic tension is all very well in its place," he said, "but its place is the *middle* of a well-wrought prophecy, not the climax. One should always end on an uplifting note. The moaning minnies must remember that we are competing for the punters' mead-money."

Dr Blair was roundly cheered by the older members of the audience, although it was noted even before the desultory question-and-answer session that the hall was nearly half-empty, presumably because the *avant garde* had retired *en masse* to the bar for a pre-prandial pint. It might have been even emptier had the attractions of the seafront been more powerful, but the weather had taken a distinct turn for the worse and the sky had become unseasonably overcast. The attending official of the Amalgamated Union of Weather Forecasters cheerfully accepted the blame for his members' failure to produce a sunnier day and promised that the dark clouds would soon blow over.

The Conference Centre soon filled up again after a leisurely and conversation-packed lunch, and every seat in the Great Hall was taken by the time that Dr. Sybil Shipton took the podium. The first paper ever to be given by one of the newly-admitted lady members was a significant occasion by anyone's standards, and no one wanted to miss it—not even those prophets who had fought to the last ditch against the admission of women to the prophethood. The demonstration that had been widely anticipated turned out to be something of a damp squib; the chorus of "sit downs" and "women outs" soon died into a mere whimper as curiosity got the better of principled adherence to a lost cause.

In the event, Dr. Shipton was careful to avoid controversy, save for one or two ironic asides. Her paper was a model of rigorous scholarship, bearing upon one of the classical problems of applied astrology: the precise moment at which the sun left the House of the Chimera and entered the House of the Aepyornis. The lady's command of the recorded data was marvelously assured and her logic was devastating, although it became clear in the course of a lively question-and-answer session that none of the Traditionalists had been tempted into a change of mind.

The final session of the day featured a fine example of the kind of oratory for which prophets' conferences have always been justly famed. Dr. Jeremiah Merlin—who cut a flamboyantly dashing figure, dressed as he was in a vividly-striped seersucker tunic—proclaimed in ringing tones that the state of Atlantis was getting into deep trouble, by virtue of the economic and environmental crisis that was slowly but inexorably extending its dire grip upon the land.

"We prophets," he cried, "will be failing in our duty if we do not rouse ourselves to exceptional efforts in making a contribution to the easing of the crisis. If we are not bold enough to be part of the solution we will inevitably find that we are merely part of the problem. We must set aside mere matters of theory, however intellectually fascinating they may be. We must forget our recent differences over the admission of women to the prophethood, no matter what bitterness the interminable wrangles may have left in their wake. We must not allow ourselves to be bogged down by the interests of every petty pressure-group that slips silver into our coffers. Above all, we must not allow ourselves to be lured into the kind of prostitution of our art that seeks to tell the mass of the public precisely what it wants to hear. It is, instead, our moral duty to declare as loudly and as insistently and as often as we can that this precious world of ours is doomed—for unless we, the prophets of Great Atlantis, can convince the people of the awesome urgency of the threats that face us, they will never take the actions that are required for our salvation. Population will continue to rise, pollution will spoil the land, and our economic system will collapse."

At this point the good doctor was interrupted by loud applause, and cries of "Hear hear!" More than a minute passed before the speaker—trying hard to suppress a broad smile—could make himself heard again.

"I seem to have struck a chord," he said, mildly, "and I thank you for your appreciation. Brothers—and, I am delighted to be able to add, sisters—*this* is the awesome task that lies before us...."

Unfortunately, the Conference Centre was struck at that moment by a gigantic, and quite unprecedented, tidal wave. Not a single prophet escaped with his—or her—life.

ABOUT THE AUTHOR

BRIAN STABLEFORD was born in Yorkshire in 1948. He taught at the University of Reading for several years, but is now a full-time writer. He has written many science fiction and fantasy novels, including *The Empire of Fear, The Werewolves of London, Year Zero, The Curse of the Coral Bride*, and *The Stones of Camelot*. Collections of his short stories include *Sexual Chemistry: Sardonic Tales of the Genetic Revolution, Designer Genes: Tales of the Biotech Revolution*, and *Sheena and Other Gothic Tales*. He has written numerous nonfiction books, including *Scientific Romance in Britain, 1890-1950, Glorious Perversity: The Decline and Fall of Literary Decadence*, and *Science Fact and Science Fiction: An Encyclopedia*. He has contributed hundreds of biographical and critical entries to reference books, including both editions of *The Encyclopedia of Science Fiction* and several editions of the library guide, *Anatomy of Wonder*. He has also translated numerous novels from the French language, including several by the feuilletonist Paul Féval.